GW00702436

Issue Three

Editors
Ginny Baily and Sally Flint

Front Cover Image
iStockphoto

Printed by imprintdigital.net Exeter

Published 2008 by Dirt Pie Press

The Editors would like to acknowledge the support of the Creative Writing and Arts Department in the School of Arts, Languages and Literature at the University of Exeter.

www.riptidejournal.co.uk

ISBN 978-0-9558326-1-1

TO MUMSIE
LOTS OF LOVE

Contents

Introduction

John Burnside

Of the prose arts, the short story is perhaps the most difficult, but it is also, arguably, the most rewarding. The most rewarding for the writer, certainly – because getting something that is difficult *right*, doing it well, or at least well enough, is one of the purest pleasures human beings can experience. Yet the short story is also profoundly rewarding for its readers because, *as* readers, we love stories for their economy and their sparing lyricism, for how they make us think about time and, most importantly of all, for what they leave to the imagination, what they *suggest*. How they make space, in other words, for our active participation.

It always comes as a surprise to me, then, when people in the publishing world - editors, sales directors, critics, booksellers – tell me that the short story is not popular – or rather, that it *doesn't sell*. This is the kiss of death for any art form these days; though perhaps it was ever thus: in my experience, writing is a solitary, uncommercial and entirely asocial pursuit - an art, in other words - but publishing is a business. This is not to say that the men and women who make publishing work do not care about the art - again, in my own experience, they care deeply, doing the jobs they do in order to bring good writing and engaging stories to the widest possible readership – but nobody can publish tomorrow if today's product does not pay its way. So it is that, the market research having been done, and the sales figures having come in, most publishers do story collections, when they do them at all, in the same way, and often on similar terms, as they do poetry – that is, for love rather than money.

Odd, then, that any straw poll of any group of readers will suggest that the short story is immensely popular, in spite of its poor sales figures. Ask someone if s/he likes short stories, and s/he will reply: No, I don't like stories, I *love* them. Yet if we look on that person's shelves, there may be very few short story collections and most of what is there will be classics, or anthologies. Something is out of kilter in our attitudes to the story and with our purchasing habits. We are, in short, missing something.

Luckily, there are people out there who are trying to address this problem. Book Trust, for example, are aggressively pushing the short story as a form, and encouraging story writers to continue working in a difficult market. Magazines, from *The New Yorker* — always a beacon in short story publishing and the one sure must-have publication for its stories alone — to local and regional labours of love and good judgement here and elsewhere, actively seek stories from new and established writers. And this book, a treasure trove of storytelling that will, by turns, move, amuse, surprise and challenge you, is as good a place to start as any, in thinking again about this marvellous, challenging and supremely beautiful art form. As Emily Dickinson says: 'Forever is composed of nows' - and every story is its own little now, providing, through the local and the fleeting, a glimpse into the vast fabric of eternity.

Evelyn Bess

Gordon Collins

The bedsit is extremely bare. The shelves are bare. No books or TV. There's just a simple wooden table and an old tea crate for a chair. The crate has metal edges and 'BEST CEYLON LEAVES' printed on it in diagonal lettering. There's a metal plate and a knife and fork on the table and tinned food on the draining board of the kitchen unit. The grey carpet is worn in many places but particularly on a strip which stretches from the window to the door. The bed is a mattress on the floor, neatly made with a clean sheet, a blanket and a single pillow. The walls are all painted white, not a shade of white. There's no post, not even junk mail. There's nowhere to sit except the tea crate. There's nothing in the crate, I checked.

There's nothing else, except for in the cupboard. I've got my things in there: toilet paper, razor, soap, pad of A4, sticky labels, pens, freezer bags, penknife, a carrier bag full of dirty tins, a white shirt and dark trousers, black socks and a trench coat with my wallet, my mobile and my watch in the pocket. I'm in my underwear so that I don't leave any clothes fibres while I search.

*

This morning I woke up crying again. I'd been dreaming of her: Evelyn Bess. She'd become a giant who carried me in one of her hands. She played with me, letting me up on top of one finger, then twisting me down into her palm again. Eventually, she reached down and put me into a hospital and left me there, saying she'd come back soon, maybe after Christmas. She left me to the sadistic nurses and the smell of ether.

Horrible business. Still, it serves me right for thinking

about her yesterday. That's not helpful. There's no time for thoughts like that. I've got an investigation to carry out and I'm determined to do it properly, not like the uninterested police or the hopeless detective I hired. They're meant to be professionals but they just tramped through here with their dirty shoes and of course they didn't find anything. I need to be much more rigorous. I need to be as detailed as I was when I first got here last week, when I did the walls and the fixtures and went half mad staring at the ceiling. Now I've just got the carpet to do. It must be in the carpet.

I've cancelled my appointments and switched my phone off. I've got enough tinned food to keep me going for five days. I've marked the carpet out with the tape into a grid of 33 numbered sections and now I'm going to pick through one section per hour, and have a twenty minute break in between so I don't lose my concentration.

Ok, let's start. I kneel down, focus and start picking through square 1 with my penknife. It goes well: several crumbs, a small piece of plastic, some hairs - unidentified but quite dark and so they might be hers. DNA testing will tell for sure later.

Section 2 is near the kitchen area and so there are all sorts of crumbs and bits of skin and mould. I get a piece of green fibre, definitely vegetable, possibly broccoli and a reddish stain, which I lift with my penknife only to discover it is ketchup – the scourge of kitchen forensics. I note down everything and put the evidence and notes in freezer bags, which I annotate with the number of the square under investigation and the time.

Section 3 has a pen top but nothing else. Recklessly, I skip to section 7, an easy one since it's in a little visited corner of the room. Just hairs really – mine I think. I have to catalogue these too, though, in order to eliminate myself from the investigation. You think about these things when you spend hours staring at the carpet. Tiring work. I'll take a break now.

*

It's evening when I become aware of the time. I have been

standing by the window for the last four hours, taking in the comings and goings of an inner city landscape but now I could not tell you a thing that was happening outside. The neighbouring tower-blocks, the road and the corner shop have absorbed me as though there was nothing else in the world and yet I couldn't describe them to you.

I pick a hair from my head. I can't see the difference between my hair and those from sections 1 and 2. This investigation is going nowhere. I empty freezer bag 1 over section 13 and freezer bag 2 over section 9. If it does come down to it, then I'd like to see some sharp—witted barrister explain why there's broccoli by the bed.

Why did she leave? She was living here, in this bedsit I bought for her. She moved in and then she left. She left two weeks ago. She only spent two days here: thirty seven hours. I came to see her on the second evening and found a note over there on the table, 'I'm sorry Max but I have to go. I'm so sorry. Do take care.'

All her numbers had been cut off. She'd left her waitress job at the restaurant where we'd met and hadn't appeared at her art college for three weeks, even though she had finished her exams and her final-year show was to be next week. I had no other way of getting to her. We didn't have any mutual friends. I had met her parents and her brother once at a restaurant but, apart from them, we didn't have a single person in common. Of course, I couldn't show her to my lot and she wouldn't introduce me to hers. Instead, she told me their names and challenged me to find them. She was like that.

After she disappeared, I spent two days going out of my mind and finding out that there was no way of tracing her and then I spent a week doing I-don't-know-what. I walked around London, I suppose. I don't know how I spent the hours. I sat in cafés, or on the train, or visited galleries in the hope of seeing her there. I would sit and watch ancient gods entwined with heroes and plump beauties in rural paradises. It meant nothing to me. Why are these paintings important? Why don't they just hang a toilet brush or a piece of meat? She could have told me why. I just walked around London, taking more and more risks crossing the road. Would she visit me if I were in hospital?

All that time, the voice in my head pounded away at me with the same question, 'Why did she leave?' It kept pushing me through all the possibilities. She realized she didn't want me? She was dying and wanted to spare me the pain of nursing her? She was brain-washed by one of her cultish friends? She had found someone else? She was tied up in the cupboard and I, in my crazed condition, had blanked out the memory of putting her there? For a while I was fixated on one explanation: she had been kidnapped by her parents. They were traditional types and, even though they tolerated most of her eccentricities, they didn't approve of her being with someone fifteen years older, and neither did they approve of me buying her a bedsit so that she could leave home. For a while I was sure that they had taken her from me, but I was desperate then and would believe anything.

Eventually I realized that none of these explanations were satisfactory. No, there was something else: the emptiness of her note, her leaving college and work so suddenly, the lack of mutual friends. She had disappeared too perfectly. She wouldn't do that to me, even under pressure from her parents. The clue was not in the evidence itself but in the lack of it. She had set a puzzle. She was testing me to see if I could, if I would, find her.

It sounds crazy unless you know her but that was how her mind worked. It was part of her art, not in a wanky student sense, but really a part of the way she found herself in the world. She worked in puzzles. Her pieces were full of snippets of text and visual puns. She signed them with scraps of OS maps with features that resembled her name. She put a crossword puzzle in one piece and the answers were the titles of her other pieces. Her tutors wet themselves over that one. She was never happy with a straightforward explanation. She found it patronizing. 'It can't be that simple,' was her catchphrase. Everything was imbued with the mystery of life and, where it wasn't, then she would imbue it. Everything from her cryptic shopping lists to her art, her eyes and her lovemaking.

Now she had set me a puzzle to find her, to see if I would come through. She had led me here, through the labyrinth of her heart. Could she be so cruel? Yes, and I can't blame her either. After all, I had been testing *her* ever since we met. I would have proposed by now, but I had never quite trusted her. In my position, as wealthy as I am, I need to be careful about marrying someone fifteen years younger and, beside that, undeniably more attractive than I ever was. It didn't matter how much I felt I loved her, I was never convinced that she loved me. All that mysterious stuff, it was alluring as hell, but could it have been a smoke screen? People will do anything for money. I've seen it.

She knew I had money, but she didn't know how much. I wanted to make sure that she would stay with me anyway. That's why I bought her this crappy bedsit instead of an apartment. Now it's all I have of her.

The bedsit is the only lead. She has turned the tables and is testing me now. She has me crawling around the floor in my underwear and I'll do it for her. I'll do anything.

I pick up the spilt evidence. I can remember which bit goes in which bag, the hairs, pen top and broccoli anyway. I put them back, get back down on my hands and knees and stare deeply into the carpet. She must be in here. She has somehow encoded herself into this carpet – whether it be deep in the fibres or in the sway of the nap or just brushed on the surface. I will find her.

Nothing much to report from squares 3 to 6. There's just a shorter hair - unidentified - and a bit of paper with a serration, probably a part of a stamp. After two hours I'm doing square 8. Now I'm absorbed in it, it's easier. Now I know which bits are evidence and which bits are just carpet or the millions of tiny flecks of paint from the ceiling or the skirting board. I know how long my concentration can last too and I'm sure to take breaks after every quarter of a square and a bigger break at the end of a square.

Another hair. That's forty two now – averaging five and a quarter hairs per square – and a lot of them are dark or red like Evelyn's. Other, more exciting finds are a tiny piece of plastic, perhaps from a button and a scrap of paper, no more than a few fibres. This one's done. I seal the bag, sit up, breathe twelve breaths and then take two steps forwards on my knees and go down deep into square 9 which is two squares into the room and roughly parallel to the end of the window. Immediately there's a short hair here and another one, a black eyelash perhaps. This square's a goldmine and here's... it's a part of a toenail clipping and, yes, it's polished black. She wore black polish and she must have had the...

Suddenly, I hear the stairs creak. I'm startled. She's come back? There's someone just outside. I stare at the door. I can actually see a key appear in the hole. The door opens. He sees me.

'Oh God, sorry.'

It's Richard, her brother. He must have been sent. I'm in my underwear, kneeling on the floor.

'I'll wait outside,' he says.

I get dressed quickly and open the door.

'I just wanted to check the post and see if everything is alright here, you know, that she didn't leave the gas on, or something,' he says and then, curiously, not accusingly, he asks, 'What are you doing here?' He looks at the carpet.

I try to pull myself together but I haven't really spoken to anyone in two weeks so I'm not prepared for this. The best I can do is not to give anything away. He's not about to tell me where she is but he might give me a clue if I'm observant enough. I'll let him do the talking... or I could have him over the tea chest in an arm lock and smack it out of him. Except that I couldn't. I have to keep a hat on the anger. He'll let something slip eventually. I just have to be calm. 'I'm staying here.'

'Right.'

There's a silence. He's awkward but then so am I. I realise that I'm staring straight at him and my hands are down by my sides, trembling. I put them behind my back and try to look relaxed. He looks again at the sectioned floor and this time points to it. 'What's all this about?'

'Nothing,' I say.

He looks more carefully at it and then surveys the rest of the room. 'Is there any post?' he asks.

'No. Where is she?' It's a stupid question but I can't help myself.

'Look Max, she thinks it's best if...'

'Oh does she? Does she think it's best?' I remember to stay calm. 'I'll find her, you know.'

'Don't find her. Forget about her.'

I want to lunge at him, but it won't help. He has access to her and that fact alone makes him seem powerful, almost like a god.

'Please. I'm going out of my mind here. I just want to ...' The words stop coming. He winces at me and I notice that I'm crying.

'Sort yourself out, Max. There's no chance a relationship can work now. Just forget about her and move on.' He puts the key on the table and goes.

I have to write this all down quickly. Everything. What was that thing he said? 'The gas', 'She thinks it's best...' I start to scribble it down. No. I have to see which way he goes. I rush to the window, but he's already gone. He could be watching. I rush back to the door and switch the light off. He could have left something. I switch the light back on and get back down on my knees by the door where he was standing. There's a little dirt from his feet. Did he try to cover something up here? He didn't come in much further than this. It's untainted. Turn the light off, for Christ's sake.

I sit in the dark worrying furiously.

*

It comes in waves. It's been seven hours now since he left. There have been four waves of it. In between I may have slept. It's getting light now. I wish I could drink or even smoke. My only vice is analysis.

I've written down the whole conversation but I can't get much out of it. There are no specifics. Again, as with her empty message, there is no information except the fact that it is a message without information. Still, I'll put it through the cryptography program when I get home. Once I've finished checking out the carpet.

I'm back on square 9. Now I remember I was making progress here: five eyelashes and a polished fragment of nail. There's some black threads here too – black was her colour. I smell them but they just stink of carpet but there's more hairs here, a whole clump, all in a small part of square 9. This is statistically very significant.

I carry on without breaks. I know I'm too tired to be rigorous but I can't stop. If I stop, I'll just think about her. Two squares along from her hairs, I find a tiny piece of white fluff which can only be a part of a feather, a swan feather I imagine. Then on the squares below her hairs, 13 to 17, there is a long thin barely visible stain. It looks deliberate. I don't see how you could spill something like that accidentally. If I press my finger hard I swear I can feel a little moisture. It's the most significant thing this side of the room.

I pick away at the fibres and it becomes my world — grey, dirty — not her exotic wonderland. I carry on to the end without stopping to think until I'm finished and I have to face up to what I've got: a small piece of plastic, a pen top, a ketchup stain, a piece of broccoli, a bit of a stamp, a bit of a feather, a long stain, a statistically significant amassing of hairs and a nail bit. I note down these findings on the floor-plan I made and I stare at them for a long time. What did I really expect to find?

*

I've been staring out of the window again and when I look back at the evidence, it all clicks. She's drawn a map of central London. The long stain is the Thames, the pen top is Bloomsbury, and there are the Royal parks! The broccoli is Green Park, the feather must be Hyde Park where we fed swans once? Or like a bird 'hide'? Yes, that must be it. A stamp has a picture of the Queen, the Regent, Regent's Park and they're all in exactly the right place which would put her — her hairs and nail — she's near Holborn.

I'm thrilled, scared. Really? I can't quite believe it. She left me a map? It's all so unlikely, but here it is. No, calm down. Work with the facts, only the facts. It's got to be right. I look for more. What else would she leave, Parliament? St Paul's? Something more personal? Spitalfields? The South Bank? I can't see anything in the right areas. Am I going mad here? I know what to do. I use my knife to cut out around the section with her hairs and I lift it out more or less intact. Underneath it's cork floorboard. Completely clean except for the broken glue marks. I think that I am wrong until a small piece of glossy paper falls off the underside of the carpet that I hold. It floats down to the floor and then I can see a red marking and above it, '...ery L...' It's a tube map. It was under the hairs and the nail. Slow down. I have to assume this is all a coincidence. No. What did Richard say?

'No chance a relationship can work, now.'

Of course, that was a strange expression to use and with his accent, '... chance a rela... now?' Chancery Lane! I have to go now. I may already be too late. I'll go to her and scream at her and forgive her and I'll take her back and this time I'll trust her.

Greg and Sarah

Jane Feaver

Growing up, Greg thought that Sarah hated him. She used to say he stank, that his friends were nerds. 'Gross' she'd say when he lay on his bed naked, steaming from his bath, 'you freak'. Since she'd gone to college, they'd had little to do with one another; nowadays she didn't come home more than a couple of times a year.

There were no guests this Christmas but Gran, their mother's mother. They'd just finished lunch. Bill, their dad, was concentrating hard, squirming in his seat. He cleared his throat, 'Going to find something softer to sit on,' he said, excusing himself, wiping his mouth with a holly napkin. 'Right, Mother,' he said, making an effort to raise his voice, using the table to hoist himself to his feet, 'going to join me?'

Gran was partially deaf with eyes like frosted glass. She farted as she let Bill guide her by the elbow through to the lounge.

Sarah rolled her eyes and slumped forward onto the placemat of yellow roses. She made a noise into the crook of her arm like a bee trying to get out of a window.

Last year, things had been different. Greg had Claire with him; he got to sit with her on the settee, his arm around her.

'No one told me she would be here,' Sarah'd protested to their mother in the kitchen. 'You could have said something.'

'What difference does it make?' Jean said, shaking her off.

'Tell him to stop smooching then.'

'She's a nice girl.'

Jean was fussing more than usual to find a double set of knives and forks for the table; she brought out a new pack of napkins. This was the first girl Greg had brought home.

'My girlfriend,' he'd started to say.

Jean had been unbearably attentive, exclaiming when Claire offered to help with the washing-up, giving her a tour of the cutlery drawers, the cupboards where she kept her mixing bowls and pans. It was clear that she approved: the sleek line of her hair, the neat, clacky heels, her tiny rabbit-bone ankles. Claire too went out of her way to please, extolling the Methodists who ran the youth club, the dances they used to perform as little girls in flame-coloured leotards.

'She's a lovely smile,' their mother said, full of hope, over the phone to a friend.

It was the sort of smile you learned from looking at magazines: a neat segment like a piece of orange.

'Do you like my titties?' Claire had asked Greg when they were on their own, turning towards him and offering them to him in the cups of her hands. She had the biggest boobs he'd ever seen and all he wanted to do was to touch. But he was aware of movement around the small house - pounding with desire - knowing someone would be bound to catch them.

Everything else about Claire was tiny. In her clothes the labels read 'petite' or XS. It made Greg think of her as a doll. When she sat on his knee, her hair against his chin was soft as fur; it smelt of cake.

'You take Claire up, will you?' their mother had said to Sarah. 'Show her where she's sleeping?'

Claire had been given Sarah's bed - floral sheets put on specially – and Sarah was going to have to sleep downstairs on the couch.

'His girlfriend,' Sarah said, 'Why can't he do it? He's got bloody legs.' Sarah used to swear in front of her mother just to wind her up.

The first thing Claire said to Greg when she followed him up the stairs and he'd pointed out where she'd be sleeping - parallel to him in the twin bed – was, 'I don't think your sister likes me.' She sat down on the end of the bed and gave a little bounce.

'Who cares?' Greg said, kneeling down at her feet, taking the hem of her skirt between his fingers, 'I do.'

A whole year had passed since then. After lunch and Dad had taken Gran off to Uncle Mick's, Greg had gone upstairs. Sarah was left with Jean, who was upset, clattering dishes to little obvious effect.

'He doesn't have a clue how to look after her. He won't have changed the sheets since last year.' Jean had buried her hands in a lava of water. She'd fallen out with her brother over Foot and Mouth. Mick had given up on farming, selling off the livestock, letting out the land from the farm that had been in the family for generations. He was intent now on converting the barns into holiday lets. And to rub her nose in it, he'd got Greg out there, helping him over the summer, practically living there with that girl Claire.

Jean couldn't bear to be in the same room as him. At Christmases, they'd agreed to ferry Gran between them.

'Is that it?' Sarah said.

'You can go,' her mother sighed as if she were on her hands and knees. But before Sarah could escape, she added pointedly, 'Incidentally, you can always take them back.'

Sarah began to fold the tea-towel, half on half, and then again, until it was a small square in her hands.

'*Marks* are good about giving your money back. You could swap them.'

'They're fine.'

'I wasn't sure if they were your sort of thing – I never know nowadays.'

Her mother was like a goat at a fence. Sarah had already buried the knickers at the bottom of her case. Ten pairs of sturdy, pink, thermal shorts.

She said, deliberately cool, 'It won't change who I am, you know - if that's what you mean.'

Jean blenched, shaking her hands over the sink, the skin tingling as if it would dissolve. 'Do you think I'm stupid?' she said in her quavery voice. 'You think I'm so ignorant, don't you, miss high-and-mighty.'

'Oh God. Will you leave the knickers out of it?'

'I can only try, you know. I try my best to understand.'

'Can we leave it for today, please?'

*

Greg was lying flat on his back, cupping a hand over the zip of his jeans, watching a fat winter fly work its way around a brown spot on the ceiling. He'd eaten too much, burping Brussels sprouts and bitter tinned chestnuts. His gums were jangling. He worried constantly about his teeth. He was thinking in circles, the minute repetitions of a fly's manoeuvrings: how last Christmas it had all been ahead of him, creeping upstairs that night after everyone else, pulling the bedroom door softly to, crouching in here, where Claire had been lying, in his new pyjamas. He'd been nervous, reaching his hand under the quilt and stroking what he decided must have been her knee. Her eyes were closed but, without a murmur, she reached down and moved his hand up against her nylon knickers so that he could feel the scratchy press of her like a swallow's nest. He'd kept completely still, as if his hand had been glued to her.

When Sarah put her head around the door, the fly dropped and began buzzing angrily in a clot of dust. The room stank of his aftershave. She sat down on the mattress and the headboard rocked against the wall.

'Feel,' she said after a while, hoiking up her sleeve and making a fist. 'Pure muscle, that. You should try it - a good work out – it'd take your mind off things.'

It was no surprise to Greg that Claire and Sarah hadn't got on. They had nothing in common. Sarah scoffed at make-up. Claire told him that his sister was stuck up. Just because she'd been to college didn't make her any better - and the way she read the newspaper, showing off.

Greg had resolved not to tell her anything; he didn't want to give her the satisfaction or the ammunition. Sarah continued to hold her arm under Greg's nose until, grudgingly, he touched the skin there. It was taut but soft, pliable as plasticine. The smell was plasticine too. He was tempted to say he wouldn't want a girl he was going out with to look like that. But instead he made a shrug of approval.

Sarah had been pretty as a child, thick, white-blond hair. Jean brushed it every morning and put it into two long plaits. On her fifteenth birthday, Sarah'd gone to get her ears pierced in the Salon in the arcade, and, on a whim, let them crop her hair at the same time. When she came home, Jean cried. She'd had it short ever since.

Where she'd been slight as a child, she was sinewy now. She carried herself better, taller. She wore a dark blue puffa jacket which she'd got in Camden market, a pair of black Levis and an old pair of suede hiking boots. She'd never possessed a pair of proper girls' shoes.

In London, she belonged to a gym. She did kick boxing and weights. 'It's addictive', she said, making a concerted effort with Greg, 'you should try it.' All that training had emphasized a line of muscle, thick as cable, from her shoulders to her neck. When she came home, she said, she got withdrawal symptoms.

Greg knew that Sarah must have known Dave Pilton - everyone did. He was a flash git, right from primary school; he'd got a girl pregnant in year nine. 'Fanny magnet' is what he called himself.

Greg wasn't going to tell her, and yet it was there at the front of his brain like oil on water. Remembering how Claire had persuaded him to go out to *Heroes* with a gang of the girls from work. She'd promised she wouldn't make him dance, that he could sit and watch them from the bar.

Sitting high up on a black plastic-topped stool, he'd felt precarious. Because of the high rainfall that summer, the basement was full of the stench of the river which ran alongside; the strobe lighting - red, yellow and green – was making his heart race; he'd drunk too much. His limbs juddered when he got to his feet.

Dave was on the dance floor with some of the soldiers from the camp. They were lairy, arms about each other's shoulders. Dave was tall, like a great ape, thrusting his pelvis, arms stretched out, a half-empty glass extended in one hand. And Claire wasn't going anywhere, she was in his orbit, in her white stilettos killing herself laughing, sticking out her tits.

Greg had pushed his way over and tried to scoop her up – a child in a riptide - shouting something into her ear above the throb of the music. But she was shaking her head and pulling away from him: she didn't want to be rescued.

'Suit yourself,' he'd said, enraged suddenly and backing off as all the lights turned red. He made for the exit, walking like you'd walk on a ship that's twisting the line of a wave. Then he groped along the powdery bricks of the wall outside, around the corner, and threw up in a pile of cardboard boxes.

He felt better once he'd been sick; but then he felt worse. He felt like crying. 'Little bitch,' he heard himself saying in a voice that sounded high and unbroken.

*

'Fancy going out?' Sarah said after a while. Greg looked at her blankly.

'Come on,' she said, getting to her feet decisively. 'We'll go mad if we stay in here.' She arched her back and stretched her arms, as if there was no significance in the fact that this was the first time she'd ever asked him to go anywhere with her.

Though it was never as wild as where they were brought up - which was higher up on the edge of the moor - it was wild enough. You could hear trees hissing down by the river and the wind whistling up the street like it was blowing across bottle tops. There was a tin can rolling this way and that outside the butcher's. Under each of the street lamps there was a flag of horizontal drizzle.

'Where'd you want to go?' Greg asked.

'Not the Lamb,' Sarah said.

'Let's go up the hill.'

They clenched their arms against their bodies, tucking their hands in under their armpits and buried their chins into the collars of their jackets. At the top, they stamped their feet and pushed through the gold and brown swing door of the *Red Lion*.

'Freezing down here,' Sarah said, 'bloody freezing,' unwinding her scarf and looking round to see if there was anyone she recognized.

It was always gloomy in the lounge bar. There was the glow from the fire, and spots of fairy lights, enough to see that there were odd groups of people sitting at tables, some of whom swivelled round crossly in the draught from the door.

As soon as his eyes adjusted to the light, Greg recognized Les Bradstock. Les was such a regular he had his own chair by the bar and a polished tankard for his beer. By the shape around the tops of his calves, Greg could tell he was wearing his britches and on his long feet, the weird, fancy brogues.

'All right?' Les gave Greg a sort of salute with his hand. He was looking Sarah up and down and nodded curtly to acknowledge her. He'd got a prickly blond chin - his moustache tipped orange from the tobacco he smoked.

'What're you having?' Greg asked.

'Good of you,' he said, lifting his tankard. 'Cheers.'

'Needed to get out,' Greg said. 'They're driving us mad.'

'Christmas - load of cod's wallop,' Les snorted.

'Les knows Dad,' Greg said by way of introduction. 'They were at school together.' He tilted his head towards her, 'This is my sister, Sarah.'

'I'm parched,' Sarah said, accepting a glass of cider and lifting it to her lips. 'Cheers'.

Les raised his glass but said nothing, looking askance at her, taking in the jeans, the boots, the hair.

'You can tell you're related,' he said finally, gathering the bubbles from his moustache with the tip of his tongue. Greg was getting hot - sweating from climbing that hill, the heat of the fire.

He wasn't mad about standing talking to Les, not with Sarah there. After Claire had gone, he'd started coming more regularly to the pub. Mick had let him stay on in the barn, but it wasn't the same on his own. He'd let the place get squalid - a week's worth of washing up in the sink, spiders everywhere - and going out was his one way of keeping at bay the inevitable retreat back home, though it came soon enough - the temptation of being cooked for, his laundry washed and ironed.

The regular crowd in the Lion was at least a generation older than Greg: Trigger, Mac, J.P, they'd appear together and lap against the bar like a creature with three heads. He'd got into the habit after a few pints of letting off about Claire. The impulse even to mention her name, was irresistible, like fitting your hand through a hole in a standing stone.

'Carrying on was she?' Les had asked once. 'Lot of it about.'

Until he voiced it, direct like that, Greg had kept the suspicion to himself. But it was there, like a trap in a wood. The way she'd brazen it out, when it was written all over her face; how once, he'd only had to get her in the door of the barn and they'd fall on each other, her breath coming in fits and starts like a small picket gate on its hinge. Now she wouldn't let him near.

It was Dave who eventually came to get her, arriving in his white van. Greg had wanted to hurl a rock through the retreating rear window, crack him on the back of the skull and watch the van career over into the ditch and upturn, rolling over, ignite into a ball of fire like you got from an oil well - one that left no trace, no skin, no bone...

'The minute you think it, believe me, they're at it,' Les had said, 'sure as eggs. They're all bitches in the end. Stick to the feathered variety, boy - they won't let you down.'

*

'You left us, then - lure of the city lights?' Les was saying to Sarah.

'I went to college,' Sarah said matter-of-factly.

'Couldn't wait to get away, then?'

'Yep. Soon as I got my chance. That was me: gone.' She shoved her glass along the bar to demonstrate.

'Well done you,' Les said. 'Going to rescue your brother from us?'

'Does he want rescuing?'

'He's had a lucky escape.'

'I know,' she said.

He could hear Sarah calling Claire *a man's girl*, like the other girls at school she despised who sat in the common room putting on mascara and lip gloss.

'Saved from a life of slavery,' Les said sardonically.

For a while, it looked as if Sarah and he were getting on like a house on fire. Greg stood as if he were listening, but in fact, as so often happened when he stood in the gloom of the bar with a drink in his hand, he was thinking of Claire.

'Drink?' Les asked him for the second time.

'Sorry. Yes, thanks. Broadside. Ta.' Greg was feeling hot again. He pulled at the zip of his fleece. And if he couldn't quite picture her face, he still kept a photograph of her in his wallet, a passport photo - big panda eyes. When he looked at it he was reminded sometimes of the incongruously harsh things she said: stories she picked up at work, like the time she told him the girls had seen a man jerking off in a window across the road; or how one girl, Sue, was on her second abortion.

When Sarah went to the loo, Les raised his eyebrows and indicated sideways as the door swung shut: 'I'd forgotten you had a sister.'

'Yeah,' Greg said.

'Nice girl.'

'She's all right,' Greg said.

'I never said a word.'

'She lives in London.'

'Enough said.'

Sarah came back into the room. She was smiling at Greg in a way that made her seem for a moment like someone he didn't know. She wiped her hands on the thighs of her jeans and got back up onto the stool, then stood up on the bars across the legs of it as if she were standing forward on a horse and peered over at the barrels of beer ranged on the floor behind the bar.

'Know your beers, do you?' Les asked.

'I'm not an expert.'

'Did you know there's a beer called 'Offa's Dyke'?'

Sarah kept her position for a minute and then sat back on the stool.

'Strange the names they come up with. There's no telling. In the Best Beer Guide, though, this pub,' he said, raising his eyebrows.

'I did grow up here,' she said.

Perhaps it was just that there was a female among them, made everyone behave a bit differently. Les's skin twitched around his mouth. Greg looked at his sister more objectively, the botched piercing at the top of her right ear, a rim of red that had swollen in the gristly runnel to her lobe like an insect bite.

'What do you do, in London?' Les asked.

'Work for the Council. Housing.'

He seemed to consider this, taking a slow slurp of his beer, then he smirked, 'Bet you've got a colourful waiting list.' He snorted, 'Soft touch, this country.'

Greg felt a prickle at his neck and lifted his hand to scratch it quiet. Sarah was staring at the polished chestnut of the bar. She lifted her chin and said levelly, 'Everyone's a right to a roof over their heads.'

'One of the compensations - living down here,' Les went on, 'no coloureds.'

He knew he'd riled her; he had a waiting-game smile on his face.

'Do you want to know why I left this place?' Sarah said, turning on her seat.

'Let's go and get a table,' Greg mumbled, his windpipe tightening. It was him who had to live here. *Give it a rest*, he wanted to say to her.

'Really nice talking to you', she said, pressing her words down so there'd be no mistaking the irony.

'Up the workers,' Les muttered, lifting his glass to their backs.

'Cunt,' she said under her breath as they reached a table at the far end of the snug. 'Ignorant git.'

*

Ever since she was a little girl, Sarah'd been skinny. Greg had been the plump one. She was skinny and fast. She could run for miles along the sand at Welcombe and he'd never keep up. She was fearless. It was always Greg who kept a weather eye on just how far away they were, making sure he could still see the two dots of their parents' heads against the canvas windbreaker. In those days, they were both naked on top, wearing matching long safari shorts. When they first arrived, they would skip with their father to the edge of the sea. He wouldn't be hurried. He'd pace it out as if he were conducting a survey. Then he'd stand, knock-kneed, dig his toes into the soggy sand, leaning backwards with his hairy belly as if he were having a wee. Their mother would have taken half an hour to get undressed, directing her husband irritably to shield her from the tug of the wind or from gangs of teenagers pattering and shrieking towards the water. Then she would sit and not move from her spot, leaning out like a rower to sort through the sandwiches and the crisps.

Sarah had found a strip of seaweed and was using it as a whip. She trailed it after her and every now and again, to keep him on his toes, would crack a line through the air. Greg was her sea horse. She drove him to the frayed metal edge of the sea. He knew that if she decided to drive him further, he would have to go. All that would save him were the plans he'd have rehearsed in his head: at the last moment, he'd reel away, duck under the waves and tunnel between her legs - even though it meant putting his head under the water - to escape her.

By the end of the day they'd all changed colour. Their father's skin went pallid like greaseproof paper. The bags under their mother's eyes, the tip of her nose were magenta. Greg and Sarah were pink with calamine lotion, like two natives from the same tribe, stinging, smeared in a way that marked them out from every other child on the beach.

Greg was wondering if Les was right about them looking like brother and sister. The school photographs that were kept on the dresser - the peacock blue of their blazers, their stripy ties - where Sarah was forced to put her arms around his waist and said she'd held her head back at that strange angle because she thought he had nits.

'Offa's dyke', Sarah tutted indignantly, dipping her fingers into a splash of beer and pushing shapes out of it, 'Did you hear him? So original. So funny.'

'What're you talking about?'

'What do you think I'm talking about?' she said, exasperated.

He saw contained in her face a neater version of their mother: the light-green eyes, the weak chin, the nose that had a slight indentation on the end, like a fork mark in dough. These features had been impressed upon him from every angle since he could first recognize a nose, an eye and a mouth and he had never questioned them. But as he studied her now, like repeating a word over and over, his sense of her suddenly seemed arbitrary, based on nothing but habit.

He was burning: it was something akin to humiliation, that she'd caught him out not knowing the meaning of a dirty joke. Or anger, that again, because he was the youngest, he was always the last to know. Like when they'd had to move off the farm, or when Gran had had her bowel removed.

He hated her for making him feel stupid. What did he know about girls? He looked at his beer belligerently. Then he said, 'You've been out with boys.'

She groaned, 'Spare me.'

'But you've been out with boys.'

'So you keep saying. It doesn't mean anything. What do you think all the fuss is about?'

'You mean you've told Mum?'

'It's who I am.' She paused and then snapped, 'It makes me sick - you bring home that little slag and it's fine, it's cool. Mum can't get enough of her. Wedding bells. Pattering of tiny feet. And what am I supposed to do? Pretend I'm waiting for Mr Right? For ever? You know,' she continued, 'if you ever had the guts to get out of this dump, you'd look back and think, Christ Almighty, how did I do it? What do you have in common with someone like him?' she made a tiny flip of her eye towards Les, '- twisted bastard. You'll end up like them. Like Dad.'

'They're not all bad.'

'You've only got to scratch the surface.'

He remembered how she used to tease him, poke his stomach. *Flubber-boy.* 'I'm not like you,' was all he said.

She was on the edge of her seat, hunched over, knitting her fingers together. 'I know that.' But then she said as if she were wheedling a child, 'We're not so unalike, you know. Not when it comes down to it. We get hurt. We fall in love.'

Greg flinched. Out loud the word sounded embarrassingly undressed. And yet, it sparked in his brain like a wire chewed in an attic.

'If you really want to know,' Sarah said, changing tack impulsively, 'I've met someone. I'm living with her. She's sharing my room.'

He didn't know what he was supposed to say. Somewhere in the hollow of his head there was an echo sounding, *Claire, Claire.*

'It's the first time - the first time I've been happy in my whole life.' Now she was glaring at him.

He was grief-stricken, panicking. *Claire*: somehow he was holding onto her in the water between them. One of their endless battles about what was hers and what was his.

'She was an air head,' Sarah said, picking up her glass and finishing what was left in it, 'forget her.'

He shrugged. Then he said, because it was the easiest and only thing he could think of to say, 'Want another?'

She wrinkled her nose, looking around, 'No. Not here.'

Greg was relieved. She didn't seem to care who could hear her. She got up and pushed her chair in, sauntered over to the bar, standing at the opposite end to Les, who was stroking his tankard, ignoring her. She dug in her back pocket and pulled out some notes to settle up.

'Right?' she said in a new bright voice, turning to Greg.

He fumbled for his jacket. He was looking over at Les, ready to unload an apology. Les didn't flicker.

As they hit the cold air outside Sarah said, 'It's like an experiment: the aliens have been feeding them, drip, drip, drip, on something that makes them think they're the centre of the universe. They go home, beat up their wives …'

'You can't say that …'

'Whatever the equivalent is.'

The wind had died down, the air was so sharp it made their noses run.

'Just look at the sky,' Sarah said, 'You don't get that in London. Wow.'

The moon cast their two bodies behind them, tall as lampposts, and flooded the sky with a spatter of stars, too many to pick out even rudimentary constellations.

'Spilt milk,' she said. And then she made a sour face, imitating their mother, '*No use crying over spilt milk* - when anything went wrong. *Anything*. She should take a spoon of her own medicine.'

He remembered them sitting in the dark together with

the TV on, watching *Star Trek* after school. Their mother would bring them beakers of milk and a plate of marmalade sandwiches.

'That's how I think of it when I come home. Like visiting another planet. I feel sorry for you Greg. There's more to life.' She ran with a spurt of energy down the hill as if she could barely contain herself, then stopped and turned back to face him as he caught up with her, 'You could come to London. You'd easily find work.'

'Maybe I'm all right as I am.'

'There's plenty more fish in the sea. You're not even bad looking.'

He was right next to her when she said that and his stomach contracted.

And then the noise, electronic and insistent, sounded like the *ting-ting* of a bell as if to break them apart. Sarah patted her pocket and pulled out a phone. As she touched it the display lit up her face. There was a message, which she tapped open. She smiled reading it, then slipped the phone back into her jacket.

Greg looked at her.

'Just someone,' she said, tapping her nose with a finger. She skipped ahead of him in her excitement, throwing her head back to address the sky: 'Beam. Me. Up.'

*

When they got home they could see by the car that their father was back, but it wasn't long before they gathered that Gran had come back with him too.

'One of you is going to have to sleep on the couch,' their mother fussed in the hallway, taking their coats off them like she did when they came back from school. 'Greg? Mick wasn't there. Do you know what he's up to? Your Gran's upset. Not surprisingly.'

Through the door into the lounge, Gran was sitting in their father's chair with her coat on and her shiny black handbag poised on her knees. 'I'm too old for this,' she was saying to the room. 'I'm past it.'

Greg and Sarah followed their mother into the

kitchen.

'Talk to your Gran,' their mother hissed at Sarah, shooing her back out into the hall, 'Talk to her, make her feel at home.' And then she said to Greg, 'He thought he was having her Boxing Day, that's what he said. Did he say that to you? He knew perfectly well. So why doesn't he ring? You'd think he'd come over and apologise at least. She's his mother!'

'I know nothing,' Greg said and walked back into the lounge.

'Gran? You all right?' Sarah was saying, kneeling down next to her.

'You're a good girl,' Gran said, the skin hanging loosely from her neck. 'I always said you were a good girl. But I'd like to see you in a skirt. On Christmas Day. How about that? Just once. It'd suit you. You've got my legs.'

'That's right, Gran,' their mother said, loudly, coming through from the kitchen with a dish cloth in her hands, 'she should show them off more, shouldn't she?'

Their father was shuffling about in his slippers, out of sorts because Gran was sitting in his chair. 'What do you want for your birthday?' he said to Sarah arbitrarily clearing his throat. 'Two brackets and a plank of wood?'

'Not now, Dad,' their mother said, flashing her eyes at him, watching her grown-up child squatting like she used to on a beach, drawing for herself a giant mermaid. 'You'll only start her off.'

Perfection

Kate Dunton

It's some kind of crazy samba music that floats out into the garden from the house. I watch him from the terrace, jokily shaking his shoulders and hips, propelled by an alcoholic joy across the grass, infinitely open to suggestion, like a spinning top waiting for the merest touch of a finger.

'Why don't you take your shoes and socks off - feel the wet grass under your feet?'

One shoe flips into a hydrangea bush, shaking the large papery blossoms that glow in the light from the conservatory. The other kicks high into the air before landing in the middle of the lawn. Then come the socks, brief white streaks in the darkness.

It's a beautiful night. Fat drops of water still drip from the leaves. The moon has come out again and there's a strange milky light coming up from the river at the bottom of the garden. The air is fresher now, after the downpour, but still warm. I breathe in the animal smell of the surrounding farms, like heat generating inside a damp bale of hay.

I follow Tim down towards the river, enjoying the feeling of my high-heels breaking through the flattened grass and plunging into the earth beneath.

'Jo! Look what you're doing!' Tim's eyes widen, the whites glinting in the moonlight. I look back at the track of stiletto holes I've made across the Marchants' lawn.

'Oops!'

'You're such a pillock, Jake,' He took to calling me Jake when we were about thirteen. I started to call him Flossie in return.

I take off my shoes and throw them at him, the first one misses, but the second hits him on the thigh. He jumps backwards to take the force, then grabs the shoe and makes as if to throw it in the river.

'Go on then.' I turn away and start trying to cover up the holes in the lawn. I hear him lob the shoe up into the tree but I don't care; it'll drop down again. If it doesn't, he can bloody well climb up after it.

'I wouldn't bother about the lawn.' Tim finally comes over. He crouches down beside me and whispers: 'Richard and Melissa are arseholes.'

'Not *arseholes*,' I say.

'Yes! Yes!' he insists, shaking his head. 'Monstrous, terrible arseholes – all of them.' He leans in a bit closer. I smell the beer on his breath: boy smell – like pickles. 'You know that woman?'

'What woman?'

He pauses, confused. 'All of them.' He throws his arms out loosely. 'With their Barbour jackets and their four-wheel drives, just so they can go and buy their ready-meals from Waitrose.' Then he gives one of his sudden in-and-out sighs, like a child who's said too much in one breath.

We've been invited to the Marchants' house for an after-show party, some dreadful Alan Ayckbourne thing about trousers and a vicar. I don't mind them, really. They've always been quite kind to me. I think they're quite pleased to have some 'young blood' in the society. They can be a bit disturbing though – all that married banter. Like earlier in the evening when I went out into the kitchen to get another drink.

'Melissa's the older woman!' Richard was opening a 'Cab. Sav.'

'Only by eighteen months,' Melissa said, pretending to be annoyed. She was slicing lemons for the G & Ts.

'You like an older woman, do you?' Penny Sharpe teased him, her smile soft and insinuating, like the movement of a cat around your legs.

'Yes – they're more grateful,' Richard's voice thickened. You could tell he'd said it before.

'Grateful for what *little* you have to offer?' Penny shot back, quick as a flash, swishing her silver-blonde bob.

'Well, it's not *that* little, Penny,' Richard said.

Melissa shoved a dish of cut lemons into his hands. 'Yes, alright Richard, that's enough!'

We give up trying to repair the holes in the lawn: time for Jake and Flossie to make their escape. I find one of my shoes, then remember the other one's still up in the tree. There's a breeze coming up from the water and the white undersides of the leaves shudder. We spot my shoe, hanging by one of its thick silver straps, right out in the furthest branches and directly above the river.

'Well, you'll just have to go in,' I nod at the river. 'I'll climb up the tree and shake the branch - you catch the shoe when it drops down.'

Tim's looking at me suspiciously, but I can see he feels guilty. I hold his eye until he throws his hands up in a shrug: 'OK, OK.'

I nip back into the house and pinch a small towel from the downstairs loo. When I come back, Tim has taken off his trousers and is wading up to his thighs about a foot from the bank.

'That's no good,' I say. 'You need to get right in.'

Tim takes off his shirt, balls it up and throws it to me. I can't help noticing how muscular his arms and chest have become, although his skin is still perfectly smooth. It's only Flossie, I remind myself. He folds his arms across his nipples, flat and brown like wood knots, and contemplates the water.

'You're not going to swim in your pants are you?' I say - on a roll now.

'Why not?'

'It'll be horrible when you have to put them back on.'

Tim wades back and climbs up onto the bank. I turn my back to him.

'Don't peek,' he says. Attention seeking, as usual.

'I won't.' I pretend to sound bored.

His pants land softly by my feet. I bundle them up triumphantly in the towel with the rest of his clothes. I hear him plunge into the water, barking like a dog and gasping for effect. When I turn, I see his head moving out into the river, the reflection of the moon breaking into slivers where his hands and feet paddle beneath the surface.

'It's actually quite nice when you get used to it,' Tim shouts. 'Why don't you come in?'

'I have to shake the tree,' I say, importantly, and start to climb the furrowed trunk. I edge out as far as I can, then lean my hands against the main branch that feeds the smaller branches where the shoe is dangling. I start rocking it backwards and forwards. Tim is just below, treading water. A few leaves drop down. I can see them on the black surface floating away from him. Finally, the shoe drops down and splash-lands about three or four feet from where he's waiting.

'Shit!' He surges forwards. Miraculously, the shoe bobs back up, but is immediately carried off by the current. Tim swims after it, his face turning in and out of the water with each stroke, cutting blades of creamy light into the oily blackness. He's soon swept beyond the boundary of the garden. I drop to the ground and grab up his things. I have to scrabble through a gap in the bushes then out onto the neighbour's lawn to keep up with him. Just as the shoe is going down, Tim reaches out and grabs it. He holds it high in the air, all excited. 'Got it, Jo, I got it!'

He hurls the shoe onto the lawn then starts to swim for the bank.

'No — not here!' I say, remembering when we were kids: the panic feeling, legs grabbed by long sucking ribbons, pulled down into the darkness. 'It's full of reeds,' I shout to him. 'Go down to the jetty and get out there.'

The jetty belongs to the rowing club. It's just beyond the hump-backed bridge, about thirty metres down stream. Tim more or less lets the current carry him there. I keep an eye on him from the bank, trespassing through all the expensive back-gardens as I run alongside. Suddenly, Tim disappears into the shadows; he must have turned his head towards the other bank and stopped paddling for a moment.

'Tim?' My voice sounds odd in the darkness.

'Yeah?'

'You OK?'

'Yeah.'

Then his face turns back into the moonlight and his arms break the surface of the water again.

The gardens come to an end and I cut through onto the small path that leads to the road. I hear Tim's lapping doggy-paddle echoing under the bridge, then a sudden sucking hush as he hauls himself up onto the jetty on the other side. I emerge onto the road and can just make out his pale figure leaning out from behind a tree.

'Throw my stuff over,' he says.

I can't resist. 'Come and get it Flossie,' I sing, in that irritating chant he uses with me, and hold his clothes above my head.

'Come on, Jake. Stop fucking about – I'm freezing.'

I roll the towel up and throw it over the road. Tim steps out, looking ghostly in the shadows, his arms raised to catch it, but just at that moment a car comes round the corner, its headlights fully illuminating his naked body. I wait for the light to slide over him and return him to the darkness, but the driver has slowed at the bend. Tim misses the towel and clasps his hands clumsily over his groin. I let out a high, excited giggle – then clamp my hands over my mouth.

I half-expect Tim to laugh too but his face is frozen. Then the car slows to a curb crawl, and the electric window on the driver's side eases down with a greasy hum. It's Penny Sharpe. She leans out and looks Tim up and down, accentuating the movement with her head to make sure he registers it. Tim bends down awkwardly and grabs the towel. The car draws level with him and Penny's hand, glinting with stagy, middle-aged jewellery, emerges from the window. We watch dumbly as her thumb and finger close ever so slowly into a circle – *perfection*. She spots me then, and laughs – as if to say 'aren't *we* lucky girls.' Then the window slides up again and she drives away.

The red tail-lights disappear over the bridge. Tim backs into the shadows and scuttles behind a tree. I cross the road and throw his clothes to him.

'You OK?'

There's no answer.

'Tim?'

'Leave me alone!'

I go and sit on the jetty; dangle my legs into the cool, dark water. I see it all again in my mind's eye unfolding in slow-motion: Tim's beautiful white body, frozen like a statue in the head-lights; the car slowing; the window easing down - and then that gesture! It wasn't even the tip of the *index* finger that Penny Sharpe had pressed down against the pad of her thumb, it was the middle finger, the *obscene* finger; morbid, somehow, like something she'd seen in the National Gallery under years of mouldering brown varnish — Cupid's fingers tweaking the nipple of Venus. And then the way she looked at me: getting my number, seeing exactly what I was up to, identifying *me* with *her*.

Tim comes and sits beside me on the jetty, rolls up his trouser legs and drops his feet into the water. We stay like this, resting back on our palms, elbows locked behind us, gently flippering our feet. We watch the moonlight catch on the ripples.

After a while, Tim splashes me with his foot to let me know he's forgiven me. I splash back. It's just that I'm not so sure I deserve it now.

Vanishing Acts

Penny Feeny

The caravan was hidden like a secret in the valley. Clasped by tentacles of bracken, it looked as though it had been planted there, sprung roots. At the sink, Sam's mother emptied a sachet of powder into a plastic bowl, squeezed out the contents of a tube and stirred the two preparations together with a wooden spoon. She had taken off her blouse; he could see the pattern of burns below her collarbone, the yellowing bruises on her upper arm. She pushed her hands first into rubber gloves, then into the paste in her bowl. She worked it into her wet hair, covered her head with a shower cap. Then it was Sam's turn. 'You always said you didn't like being ginger. Gingers get picked on.' She settled the towel around his shoulders like a cape and watched the minute hand moving slowly round her watch face. Outside in the dusk, red-skinned deer blundered into the buried yoke of the caravan and blundered away.

Afterwards, when he looked in the mirror, his hair was dark and dull as a dead animal; there was no shine to it. And the ginger freckles were still there, all over his skin, like a blight. 'You need to let it grow a bit more,' said his mother. 'To suit the clothes.' She'd picked them up in an Oxfam shop: cotton skirts and summer dresses, tops in pink, turquoise and lilac. She'd introduced him to Mrs Grant as 'My daughter Samantha.' Mrs Grant had handed over the keys to the caravan without showing much interest.

On that first night they'd fetched fish and chips and Sam's mother had unravelled the greasy newspaper, turning the sheets from side to side as if she expected to see her own face staring out at her. The morning after she'd dyed his hair, she sent him up the farm track to the village general store. Piles of newspapers were bundled on the counter beside the cartons of liquorice sticks and chewing gum. Sam, in his flounced skirt, bracelets clicking on his wrist, bought half a dozen to take back to the caravan but they found no reference to missing persons. It seemed no-one was looking for them.

His mother had been hired to do the cleaning for the big old farmhouse and the trim rows of modern caravans that, unlike their own, perched on cropped green grass with a view along the valley. She wasn't an efficient cleaner. Her mop left smears and her feather duster failed to disturb the cobwebs. She'd been better at singing. She'd once had a powerful voice but now it was locked inside her throat. She took her bucket of bleach to the toilet block and swilled it over the concrete floor until the fumes made her eyes smart and strangled any tune that might have tried to escape. Sam was supposed to help but he kept getting under her feet. 'A *girl* would be able to dust,' she complained and sent him off to wander the site – as long as he didn't speak to anybody.

*

Over the days he grew bolder. He explored the woods that led to the stream and the great empty barns at the back of the farm. Raindrops spattered on the corrugated roof. The concrete stalls were scrubbed down; only a whiff of manure remained. It conjured for Sam the ghostly cows, their anxious eyes and damp muzzles, the flick of their narrow tails – like the flick of a leather belt, a strip of cow-hide with the sharp sting of a wasp.

'What d'you think you're doing?' The girl was older than he and taller, long hair looped behind her ears, long legs in Wellington boots. She was backing him into the corner.

'Nothing.'

'You're trespassing.'

'No I'm not. I live here.'

'*I* live here,' said the girl. 'And if you're from the caravan site, this bit is private.'

'My mum works here,' Sam said.

'Oh…*her*.' Her head dipped to one side and then the other. Her feet shuffled in the boots that were too big for them. 'I'm Polly,' she said. 'I'm eleven.'

Sam stared up at the cross-beams supporting the roof. 'Why aren't there any cows?'

'Because.'

'Because what?'

'Because we have the caravans instead.' She leant forward, closed in on him until her mouth brushed close up to his ear. 'Want to share a secret?'

When your whole life is a secret, what can you tell? 'I don't know any,' Sam said.

'That's pathetic,' said Polly. 'Come on. Follow me.'

At the door of the farmhouse she kicked off her boots and tiptoed along the hallway in dirty pink socks. She felt on top of a doorframe for a key and turned it in the lock. 'We never use the dining room,' she said. 'So mum lets Frank leave his stuff here.'

'Who's Frank?'

'He's a magician.'

Large dustsheets left over from decorating covered a mystery heap of treasure. They both struggled with the heavy weight of fabric. Polly pulled out a stack of plywood and unfolded it into a series of boxes with mirrored doors. She climbed inside one of them. 'This is for making the lady vanish,' she said. 'Try and find me.'

Easy, thought Sam, tugging at the door she had pulled shut behind her. The box was empty. He listened carefully. He was sure he could hear her breathing. He was examining the sides for another way in when he heard Mrs Grant calling. Polly must have heard too, because she burst out of the box and yanked the cover down over all the equipment while Sam stood and puzzled.

'There's secret compartments,' she said. 'I'll show you later how it works.' She lowered her voice. 'We're not supposed to come in here, disturbing things. But…'

'But what?'

'See them?' She pointed to a set of Punch and Judy puppets lying head to head, their empty bodies sagging.

'Yes.'

'They're magic they are. When no-one's around they come to life, leaping about all over the place, beating each other up. You listen at the door, you can hear them.'

'I don't believe you.'

'I don't care.' She tugged a piece of hair into her mouth and chewed it. Sam wondered whether he caught Judy's skirt twitch or Punch's eye close in a conspiratorial wink. 'Anyway, I'm going to be Frank's assistant when I grow up. He's already teaching me how to do tricks.'

'So where is he now?'

'He's got a job some place.'

'Isn't being a magician a job?'

'No. It's weekends.'

'Is he your dad?'

'No. Why would you think that?'

'Because of all his stuff in your house.'

'He's just a lodger, like you. I haven't got a dad.'

'Me neither.'

'What happened to yours?'

Sam shrugged, as if the person who had *not* put their pictures in the newspaper, had *not* notified the police of their disappearance, had *not* tried in any way to come after them, did *not* really exist.

'Mine shot himself,' said Polly.

'Why?'

'Foot and Mouth.'

'What's that?'

'It's when we lost all the cows,' she said in a tone of enormous condescension, 'I guess you would have been a baby.'

Mrs Grant's voice grew louder, entered the room a few seconds ahead of her body. 'Polly. Samantha. What are you doing here?'

'I'm just showing Sam around. We're going up to my room now.'

'You haven't touched anything?'

'No, of *course* not.'

Polly's room had a TV, crowds of soft toys and discarded Barbie dolls. 'You can play with these if you like. I've grown out of them.' Inside her wardrobe her clothes fought for breathing space. With difficulty, she pulled items off hangers. 'This is too small for me, now,' she said. 'And this. And this. Do you want them? Mum said she thought you needed stuff to wear.' Perhaps she couldn't see the blush beneath his freckles. She crammed the clothes into a carrier bag. Then she said, 'I'll do your nails shall I? Shall I make up your face too?' And out came the foundation sponge, the blusher brush, the mascara wand, the lip pencil, with which she painted his skin. A mask stared back at him from the mirror. 'Your hair's a mess,' said Polly. 'I don't think I can do anything with it.'

But over the summer his hair grew and she had a knack of braiding the short pieces into one another to make it appear even longer, tying it with ribbons, treating him as if he were a life-size Barbie doll. It was a cool grey August and they spent much of it playing inside, watching DVDs, dressing dolls, baking inedible cakes. Occasionally, they'd go down to the river to build a dam and skim stones, or they'd swing on the metal gates at the back of the old cowsheds. They formed a league against the other children on the site, the ones who came and went and never settled. Mrs Grant was pleased that Polly had a companion; Sam did what he was told.

*

Coming back from the farmhouse to the caravan he heard a man's voice through the open window. Instinct flattened him against the side. The shade was so thick the metal never warmed up; his fingers pressed against the cold smooth exterior. He held his breath until he heard his mother's laugh. Her laughter made him bold. He breathed out again, mounted the steps and opened the door. Her face was flushed. She was wearing earrings that swung in giddy circles, catching the green-tinged light. 'There you are,' she said. 'This is Frank.'

'And you must be Samantha?'

Sam nodded; he could hardly hide his disappointment. He had expected someone who looked like a wizard: a tall hat, a long beard, a billowing cape. This man was well-fed, clean-shaven; small eyes darted like tadpoles behind his glasses. 'Are you Frank, the magician?'

'He's Mrs Grant's lodger, same as we are,' said his mother. 'We've got quite a bit in common.' She tossed her head and her earrings danced.

Frank said, 'Want to see a card trick?' The cards spun in the air as if they were joined together, like a concertina. They slithered onto the table in a neat heap and he was left with an ace in his hand. Sam tried to look unimpressed. Frank reached forward and his fingers closed over Sam's ear; he tensed, waiting for it to be yanked or punched.

'Pretty hair,' murmured Frank, of the braids that Polly had woven. He pretended to stroke it and then pulled back his hand. In his palm lay a huge round £2 coin. 'You should find somewhere safer to keep your pocket money, kiddo,' he said.

'That isn't mine.'

'It is now. Run along and buy yourself an ice cream.'

Sam looked at his mother. She was smiling. Behind the smile, at the back of her throat, a hum was rising, the beginning of a song. She prodded him in the side. Clasping the coin, he started down the caravan steps. 'Cute little thing,' he heard Frank say.

Later that night, curled on his bunk, knees drawn up tight to his chest, he heard a tapping on the window. His mother shifted from her bed behind the curtain. The door opened onto whispers and giggles. He put his fingers in his ears and the pillow over his head.

*

It was raining: a steady thrumming on the roof like knives thudding home. His mother was cleaning the farmhouse because Mrs Grant and Polly had gone shopping in Taunton. Sam set off along the churned-up path, battling the bracken to find her. She would tell him off for tracking mud over her clean floors, so he slipped off his shoes, though his feet still left marks on the wet stone flags, like footprints in the sand. The sink was full of saucepans soaking. The television was chattering loudly in the sitting room although there was no-one to watch it. The upright vacuum cleaner stood like a sentinel in the hallway.

Sam put his ear to the panelled door of the dining room and concentrated on the sounds on the other side. He could hear Punch and Judy sneaking into the collapsing boxes, running around on their little stage, jumping out of the giant top hat. You have to be very quick to catch them, Polly had said. He grabbed the handle and entered in a single movement.

His mother turned so swiftly the buttons flew open on her blouse. He could see her breasts hanging pale and loose. 'Good God!' she exclaimed, fastening them up. 'I thought you were Mrs Grant come back early. What on earth do you think you're doing?' Behind her, Frank was puffing and replacing his spectacles on his nose.

'It was Punch and Judy,' Sam said.

'It was what? Don't you know this room is out of bounds?'

'I wanted to see the magic,' Sam said.

Her feet were bare, like his. She was hunting for her shoes. 'Haven't I told you a million times you have to be on your best behaviour here?' Her voice rose, piercingly. 'Otherwise you know what will happen!'

Sam gulped back sobs. Frank came over and laid a hand on his shoulder. 'No worries, pet,' he said. 'I'll show you Punch and Judy if you let your mum get on with the hoovering.'

Sam's mother looked grateful. She clipped out of the room in her restored shoes and carted the vacuum cleaner upstairs. He could hear it eating up the dust in Polly's bedroom above their heads.

'Now then,' said Frank kindly. He made Sam sit on his knee and slipped the glove puppets over each of their hands. 'These two are always fighting,' he said. 'Punch is the crafty one. You can be Judy. Come on, have a crack at him if you like.'

The puppet heads dipped and wobbled. Crafty Punch was darting all over the place, groaning realistically whenever he got hit. The game was good fun until he started to sneak up the inside of Sam's leg, under his skirt. Until now their tussles had been playful, but Sam, remembering the panic in his mother's voice, could not afford to be found out.

Judy tried to bat Punch away, but Punch wasn't having

it. Judy hit out harder. Frank's breathing was louder than the Hoover; his face was glistening with tiny pimples of sweat. Punch was pinching small slices of Sam's thigh between his rubber hands and the pinches hurt. Judy gave up the battle beneath the skirt and thwacked Frank's head instead, knocking his glasses off. The action unbalanced their weight on the chair, which toppled over, and Frank and Sam landed heavily on the floor.

'Hey,' said Frank. 'That wasn't necessary.'

Sam scrambled up and flung Judy's body to the far side of the room. 'I don't want to play with puppets anymore.'

Frank rubbed his red face and looked cross. 'I hope you're not going running to your mother are you? You know how it would upset her.'

*

His mother had borrowed Mrs Grant's iron. She'd laid a towel over the little table in the caravan and was pressing her clothes. She was folding them into neat squares and rectangles and piling them back into the suitcase. 'I know you'll miss Polly,' she said. 'She's been a good friend to you.'

'Why do we have to go?'

'Because there isn't a job here anymore. The summer's over.'

'Where are we going?'

'We'll be getting a place in Taunton. I'll be working with Frank, as his assistant.' She laughed. 'You know, he's going to make me vanish.'

That was what Polly had wanted. 'You're too fat,' said Sam.

Although she had complained of long days sweeping and scrubbing, wearing out her feet, her elbows and her knees, she had found time for indulgences, for Cornish pasties, lardy cake and clotted cream. They started each day with farm eggs and bacon fried on the Calor gas stove; at night they ate fish and chips and chocolate bars.

'You little tyke! Don't be so cheeky.'

'You won't fit inside the boxes.'

'Whatever. He says he wants me with him.'

Sam felt a sudden driving panic. 'He's going to saw you in half! He's going to throw knives at you!'

'Don't be silly. He's a kind man. He'd never hurt a hair on anyone's head.' She left the iron propped on its side and came over to him. She put her arm around his shoulders and drew him close to her plump soft stomach.

'Does he know about me?'

'I'll have to pick my time to tell him,' she said. 'Don't want to give him a heart attack. But that's not your problem, so don't you worry.'

She was squashing him. He pulled away. She tried to reach out for him again but he turned and ran with his head down like a young bull. Straight into Polly.

'Watch it!' she shrieked.

'Sorry. I didn't mean to...'

A heavy hazy sun had thrown a blanket of heat over the valley. Pressure had risen and finally given them a hot summer's day. 'I'm going down to the river,' she said, and he saw she had a towel under her arm. 'Coming?'

They lay on the bank and splashed their hands in the water, breaking their reflections into a hundred tiny ripples.

'Shall we swim?' said Polly. 'I'm sweltering.' She stripped off her shorts and tee-shirt, held her breath in her chest so long that it swelled, and plunged in. Bubbles danced along the surface. Her face, rising from the water, was white with the shock of its cold grasp. Her hair turned dark, streaked onto her shoulders. 'You have to come in too,' she said. 'Loser.'

She turned and swam out to the centre of the stream, where it widened into a pool. Particles of mud stirred up from below hung suspended, clouding the water. Sam stripped down to his pants, to the rose-patterned little-girl briefs, and joined her. He had wondered for weeks what swimming there might feel like. Polly's eyes glittered; her hands beat the water into crests. He splashed back. They raced from bank to bank, though the distance was scarcely far enough for competition. They searched the bed for pebbles in unusual shapes or colours. They dared each other to dive beneath the overhanging arm of a tree. Then they got out.

Polly looked at Sam, at the knickers that had turned

transparent, at the clump of soft male flesh inside them. The tiny buds on her chest shrivelled in distaste. 'What's *that*?'

He gulped, unable to explain.

'Pervert!' she shrieked. She picked up her clothes and stalked away from him. At a safe distance she dressed, raising her head just once to say, 'You were supposed to be my friend. Why didn't you *tell* me?' She ran off without listening for his answer.

Sam picked up the girly clothes and dropped them into the stream. The water flowed into the cotton jersey and filled out the shapes to make a limbless torso. Naked, he walked at a steady pace through the tousled grass. He didn't care if any of the campers saw him. He wanted to be seen. But there was nobody around.

There was nobody in the caravan either. The suitcase was fastened with straps on top of his bunk. He undid them and rummaged through his mother's neat packing. At the bottom, he found his old jeans, the ones he'd run away in: too thick, too heavy for today's heat, too short now he'd grown, but he put them on anyway. In front of the mirror he held the scissors to his head and sliced away at the dead black growth. His mother had been touching up the roots for him but lately she'd run out of dye. The hair drifted to the floor like fur until he'd exposed the soft golden pelt of a marmalade cat.

He ran his hand across the stubble. No-one would recognise him now. He'd go up to the farmhouse and sneak into the dining room. Sam, not Samantha, would wait among the mirrored boxes, the collapsible top hats, the empty glove puppets, until Frank came back.

Doctor in the House

Paul Brownsey

My doctor turned to me at the worst moment of her life. She knocked on the door in the middle of the night, calling, 'Mr Daintree, please help me.'

Dr. Grier, Dr. R. Grier, Dr. *Rosamund* Grier (a lovely name), is not really the sort of person to have crises in her life. She has a wise, gentle smile that places all you tell her, all she sees, within a universe in which everything is working out for the best. There is dignity and sureness in all she does and says. Her knocking and calling out to me were soft, so as not to wake the neighbours.

I recognised the voice. The house was ready for her, nothing to tidy out of sight because 'it's the doctor'. I leapt out of bed and rushed downstairs in my dressing-gown. (If I trip and fall, I thought jokily, the doctor is at hand!) I opened the door to the night and there she was. I admired again the short unpretending cut of her auburn hair: Dr Grier has nothing to do with the silly anxieties of fashion. The street-lamps, still uselessly on at this deserted hour, gave her simple opal earrings a pale glow. I had verified that they were clip-ons one day at the surgery when she bent forward to study some red spots on my chest which I feared were AIDS but were merely de Morgan's spots. An intelligent woman would not make holes in her ears or, indeed, in any other part of her body.

She said now, 'When the present crisis arose, I knew that you were the one person who could help. Although we have never spoken in terms beyond those appropriate to a doctor-patient relationship, I have always perceived you to be among the most sensitive and intelligent of my patients, someone whom it would be a privilege to know on a personal level if medical ethics did not forbid it.'

This confirmed what I had long guessed. When, strapping the blood-pressure apparatus onto me or signing the prescription for my anti-depressants, she asked if I had any holidays planned, this was not the chit-chat which every doctor makes to put patients at their ease: she really wanted to know and was imagining travelling with me on, say, a Nile cruise. (David would have no right to complain, given *his* cruising.) I have often looked for her around town, for she is the sort of person who, while a superb doctor, would also appreciate concerts and plays and good restaurants, but it is a measure of her dedication to her calling that I have never seen her anywhere except at her surgery at 74 Hungerman Street; not even in Cleveden Drive, where she lives.

As she entered the sitting-room she said, 'This is *very* nice.' She is always genuinely pleased with your cholesterol level or blood-test results.

'Thank you.'

'You are not,' she continued, 'slaves to so-called style. You have an unerring instinct for what is necessary in a sitting-room to produce a tasteful, comfortable, convenient environment. It must give you and your partner such pleasure to sit here.'

'It does,' I said modestly. To say she'd responded with professionalism when I told her I was gay would be to malign her, for that suggests the false cooing you get from people in the caring professions even if they don't really like you (though with many women, of course, that isn't just the result of job-training). No, Dr Grier's approval of me and David was just part of her unerring and effortless recognition of all that was good.

I helped her off with her raincoat and hung it (on a hanger, of course) in the hall cupboard. She was wearing the smart dove-grey jacket and skirt she often wore in the surgery, just the clothes for a woman who is innately elegant. There was a faint perfume that made one think of jewels glistening from another world.

She sat down without waiting for an invitation. We were beyond formalities.

'Would you like some refreshment?'

'A small whisky with its own volume of water, please.' I admired the way in which she, a woman, could ask for whisky without bravado or false shame or need to justify. Simply, her wisdom told her that whisky (in moderation, of course) was one of the good things of the world.

She was studying the pictures on the walls when I returned. She said, 'You have excellent taste in pictures.'

Actually, pictures were more David's line. He liked going to auctions to pick up things – operative phrase, that – especially paintings by named Glasgow artists that sometimes sold for very little when houses were cleared after deaths. We were proud of two flower-pictures by someone called Mary Gunn, Rennie Mackintosh's girlfriend before Frances Macdonald. My contribution, bought (for only £30) as cover for attending an auction with David, was a painting of a young man who looked a bit like me. Dr Grier remarked that he had the noble and idealistic look of the generation that died in World War I.

After talking about pictures, we turned to the books. Mine were mainly detective stories and they looked a bit lightweight compared to David's heavy stuff - not only did he do theology at university (though without any intention of becoming a minister), but he still reads theology books now. The twists and turns seem to fascinate him, e.g. on how God can blame you or even forgive you for bad things that you did because He predestined you to do them. However, I was not going to claim these books were mine; there could be no false pretences with Dr Grier. I was rewarded when she said, 'Detective novels are the truest theology, because they crystallise more essentially than any other form of literature the eternal conflict of good and evil and the yearnings of our hearts for goodness to prevail.'

She rested and then continued, 'Of all my patients, I knew you were the one I could turn to. Gay people, particularly gay men, are so much more perceptive about human relationships than heterosexuals. And your insight is exceptional even for a gay man. So often, striving to help some patient whose real problem was not that they were ill but that they were unhappy, I have thought to myself, 'If only Mr Daintree could advise me what to say to this poor person.' I have even wondered whether to offer you employment at the surgery as a counsellor to patients: you could do them so much good.'

'Then in that capacity, Dr Grier, let me counsel *you*' - we both smiled at the joke – 'for once to think a little more of yourself and less of your patients. It cannot be something negligible that has brought you here at three in the morning.'

She said, with perfect simplicity, 'My husband tried to kill me.'

As always, I couldn't imagine a husband for Dr Grier, though of course she would have one. Any image would be too particular: he'd have to be, say, heavily built, with dark, matted hair, a harsh, sneering voice, a liking for nougat, a thumb shortened by an accident with an electric saw, a habit of saying, 'That's your problem,' whereas Dr Grier's uplifting gaze ranged dispassionately (yet with *com*passion, too) over the whole gamut of human types. Still, she would be a good wife in the traditional sense, ironing his shirts and submitting to sex, even though her own sexual desires – and let us be clear, she has them, she is a real woman – are never satisfied by him, nor could be by any mortal.

It was also impossible to imagine anyone, husband or not, seeking to kill Dr Grier. What could she do to provoke? She administered relief for pain, hope for despair, strength for weakness. She caused you to see the beauty and goodness in things.

She continued, 'The question of *how* is easy to answer. I was in bed. He had stayed up; drinking, as is his wont. Suddenly some instinct, some intuition outwith the range of ordinary human knowledge – for though I am a scientist my mind is not closed to the possibility of other modes of apprehension – made me roll from the place in the bed that I occupied. Immediately a carving knife stabbed the mattress in the place where I had been lying. My medical knowledge enabled me to cause him to stagger backwards by thrusting a finger at a vital point in his neck. In his pain and confusion I escaped from the bedroom. To think of a refuge was to think of you.'

'Thank you.'

'As for the *why* of it, I am at a loss for an answer.'

Like an Agatha Christie detective, I elicited the fact that her husband's career as a lawyer came to an end when he was imprisoned for embezzling a client's money. I said, 'His wife adorns her calling, its perfect embodiment. His career has ended in disgrace. Unable to emulate her, he has no alternative but to eliminate her.'

She would have learned of her calling as in an Annunciation painting.

She said, 'Now I understand. Thank you for that insight.' She reflected and said, 'I have loved my husband too weakly. I must strengthen my love for him, so that it may save him from such despair ever again.'

This was a new thought, that actually *loving* a bastard, not just staying put hoping for some unimaginable improvement, was something you might continue to do. Since Dr Grier did this, it couldn't be weakness, couldn't be neediness.

There was the sound of footsteps on the stairs and, after a knock, David put his head round the door, hair tousled from sleep.

'Ah, David! I'd like to introduce you to Dr Grier. I have often told you how much she has done for me.'

She held out her hand. 'I have long wished to meet you, Mr Ogg,' she said. Naturally she remembered his name from when I gave it to her for next-of-kin purposes. 'The deep bond between you and Mr Daintree is immediately evident. I often say that heterosexuals have a great deal to learn from homosexual couples.'

Except that for two years he was humping Douglas Semple on the side and it's a fucking miracle you aren't treating me for HIV infection.

'Thank you,' I said.

His striped dressing-gown, blue and white, was what a nice person would wear. The warm but respectful way in which he shook hands with her couldn't fail to impress anyone, me included, with the idea that he was someone you could envy yourself for having as a partner. When I explained why she was here, he was properly horrified and then said, 'Why don't I make myself useful by making some sandwiches and coffee? It is decaffeinated,' he added to Dr Grier, 'for we try to live healthily here – no fry-ups and always five portions of fruit and veg a day.' He exited for the kitchen, barefoot and capable.

I'd had it all planned, how to inform her of David's infidelity. I'd say, 'Dr Grier, I, too, have been on the receiving end of a stab-wound to the heart. The question of *how* is easy to answer. On Saturdays, David would go to Semple and Son's Auction Market. I confess I grew suspicious. I say 'confess' because, as I am sure you agree, suspicion is always a sin against someone one loves. I began to accompany him. He would go behind the scenes, ostensibly to enquire if any Mary Gunns were coming up. Squeezed behind a corridor door that was wedged open, watching through the hinge-crack, I saw him wait with two other men outside an office from which, in due course, emerged the son, of Semple and Son. I had already noticed that under cover of surveying the crowd for bids his eyes lingered on this or that man far longer than was necessary to ascertain whether a bid was forthcoming, though not on me. Now, like a dealer assessing items offered to him for sale, he looked in turn at the three waiting men, kissed my David on the mouth, then walked away without a word.'

I'd envisaged pausing to find the exact words for the kiss, for doctors don't like it when patients just say, 'I feel bad,' unable to describe symptoms properly. 'It was a quick kiss, but slack, with a lot of saliva in it. It had the quality of a selection ritual – Paris awarding the apple in mythology perhaps or putting a red spot on a picture to indicate it's sold.'

But now I'd seen David through her eyes, his face mobile with concern and determination to be of service, my resolution to inform on him shrivelled. He became a mere outline, a ghost at daybreak, that defiantly expressionless David who, as I tried to get through to him how awful his infidelity made me feel, shifted his eyes about the room as though looking for something; who, before I'd finished, picked up the TV remote control (dented from when pain had made me go outside and hurl it at the house) and muttered, 'Love and do what you will. Augustine.'

Vision and welling sound signalled that that was all I was to get.

Happily, this reverie of troubling memories was halted by loud thudding. I leapt to the hall and called through the front door, 'Who is it?'

'My wife's in there and I want her out.' A harsh voice, slurred.

'Go away,' I said, 'or I shall call the police,' but, before he could reply, Dr Grier was at my side.

'I'll go out and speak with him.'

'But – but – he tried to *kill* you,' I said. 'Okay, but look, we'll have him in here, in the house. Safer.'

'I couldn't possibly impose on you so far as to have such a dangerous and unstable a person in your lovely home.'

Her voice had the irresistible authority that makes us say, *Doctor's orders!* She pulled the door shut behind her, and I decided the best service I could do was to be a witness. I pressed an ear against the frosted glass of the door. There was her voice, soft, measured, an amelioration of ills, and that was his sneering rasp, but, alas, I could not make out any words except a snarled, 'That's your problem!' His voice became still more violent. Then there was silence. And then I felt a sudden crushing pain in the ear that was pressed against the glass followed by a hot pulsing as though blood was flowing from it: he had hit her. Of course she did not cry out, so as not to disturb the sleeping neighbours. Suddenly there were new sounds, grunting and thumping ones. I pulled the door open without a thought for my own safety. Struggling and gasping and lashing out, two figures rolled among the purple and ochre crocuses beneath the rose bushes.

One of them was barefoot, in a long striped garment tied with a cord around the waist that came undone as I watched; the buttocks, I realised, were David's. The other, a stranger, had got his shirt ripped open as the two twisted and struck and kicked and gouged; his bare chest was smeared with earth.

It was no good telling myself that the stranger's hair was black, thick, matted, low on his forehead, while Douglas Semple had a cloud of fair hair, curly and wispy like a little boy's. No matter that where Douglas Semple was lean as steel rods, the transient touches of his body against the fabric of his silky brown suit hinting at energy and authority, this man was

heavily built. The entwined writhing pair were David and
Douglas Semple, having sex.

'Stop it!' said Dr Grier in her doctor's-orders voice
even though she was propped against the house wall, blood
seeping down the left side of her face. Of course David
obeyed immediately, getting to his feet, hastily retying his
dressing-gown. (A doctor is used to the naked body, but
outside of the surgery ordinary modesty should prevail.) The
other man, lips a bloody mess, lay sobbing on the ground,
curled awkwardly, clutching himself as though David had
kneed him in the balls. Booze reeked off him.

She said to David, 'Thank you so much. This is a
house of courage as well as kindness.'

'Thank you,' I replied. I felt proud of him slipping out
the back door at the knock on the front, hurling himself naked
at the stranger in the nick of time. So forgetful of himself that
it broke your heart.

He was humble, self-deprecating, hobbling and
hopping barefoot on path and garden: 'If I hadn't done it
Nigel would never have forgiven me.' Someone who has been
saved doesn't necessarily want to learn that saving them wasn't
the point, but Dr Grier graciously gave no sign of noticing.
'Mr Daintree has the strength to forgive anything,' she said.
Suddenly the three of us laughed in a way that revealed perfect
good-feeling uniting us – Oh, let's give it its proper name,
love.

The blood on her face was gone. Already she had
healed her own wound.

She called for hot water and took out medical
equipment. (I forgot to mention her small leather suitcase, of
the highest quality.) Fearlessly she crouched before her bastard
of a husband, and cleaned and dressed his wounds. She
murmured the encouragements, the kind requests to move this
way and that, which I knew so well. She was the channel for all
good.

I said to David, 'Go and put something on. You'll get
your death of cold.'

'So will you,' he said. Dr Grier waved us away, and
when we returned with jeans and sweaters under our dressing-

gowns, Barry Crump (she kept her maiden name) had slunk off and she was clicking her suitcase shut.

'It would be an honour,' I said, 'to give you permanent refuge from that terrible man. Please come and live with us.'

'Even after you divorce him,' David seconded.

Her gaze was on the immeasurable distance where lay the pattern of the whole universe and everything within it. 'I shall not divorce him.'

'But he's totally betrayed your trust,' said David.

I left a pause for that sentence to resonate, then seconded: 'He's an animal, he's violent, he could do you terrible harm, you can't go back to him!'

'His failings are very great, I agree; but they do not cancel my marriage vows, and I could not violate them without losing my integrity.'

She added, with a simplicity which carried its truth to us all, 'Integrity is my strength and shield, as it is everyone's. I have learned that from you, Mr Daintree.'

Once or twice I had glimpsed, but then lost again, an obscure place of peace that existed because I had not done what David had done. This peace had nothing to do with being able to hurl stinging comparisons at him (though I do not really know if they would sting) or being smug about not having sunk so low.

But suddenly I saw Dr Grier on her back in the flower-bed, her legs waving in the air, bloody scratches on them made by our rose bushes. The dove-grey suit, rumpled and earth-stained, was rucked up, revealing her stocking-tops and the strip of bare flesh above them. She was no older than me, perhaps younger.

'Christ, she's one of those,' I said, after she'd gone.

We were in the sitting-room, drinking the rest of the coffee, eating the rest of the sandwiches, trying to incorporate the events of the night into our lives. Every now and then I would peep through the curtains as though they were still going on, though of course there was just silence and darkness.

I added, 'One of those masochists who'll put up with anything from a man no matter how appallingly he treats them.' Deliberately, as David reached for the last sandwich, I took it.

I said, 'Like those women you read about who fall for violent criminals in jail, those weird marriages. Intelligent women, educated women, psychiatrists, and they roll over at the thought of some thug with a murder conviction. So Dr Grier is one of those. Integrity – huh!'

David had been trying to interrupt and now I allowed him to. He said, 'Why must you be so cynical? I mean, in your book *forgiving him* equates to masochism and being, like, too needy to dump him as he deserves.'

He said, 'I think it's terrifically noble that she can stick to her love even though he's been such a bastard towards her.'

He'd taken hold of my hand; no, wrist, like someone feeling my pulse. The dove-grey suit was immaculate again, creases vanished, the skirt its normal length, stocking-tops unimaginable. She was back on her feet and would find it a worrying symptom if I could not show I knew forgiveness was real.

Next morning I discovered that the crocuses (how strange that their purple and ochre had been so visible in the night) weren't really crushed at all.

It became our practice, David's and mine, to keep the spare room ready for Dr Grier, just in case she should ever again need our succour. Indeed, it became a couple's private joke that she was living there, and we'd say things like, 'Turn that music down – you'll wake Dr Grier,' or, 'Dr Grier wouldn't approve.'

At the surgery, quite properly, she never alluded to that night. I'd remark, say, on the difference between the plastic spatula she used when inspecting my throat and the wooden one like a lolly-stick that doctors used when I was a boy, but that was as far as things went. She accepted my samples, of blood or urine or nail clippings, just as though she had never hammered desperately on our door and told me that I was her only hope.

The Denver Ophelia

Wendy Brandmark

Cinderella went to her mother's grave beneath the hazel tree and cried: 'Shiver and quiver, little tree, Silver and gold throw down over me.' The bird threw a gold and silver dress down to her. Grimms' Fairy Tales

Ruthie buys her clothes off the backs of other women. I say, 'My mother would die if she saw me in here.'

'But she is.' Ruthie puts up her hands. 'Dead.'

'Can you be nicer about it? It's only been a year.'

We're in the death throes, the last stages of writing our dissertations, what she calls 'our dissembling'. She's been here for five years finishing.

After hours spent gleaning and writing, we meet up in the afternoon beneath a sky blue as the virgin's dress. Dry blue with never a tear. 'Heaven's hell,' Ruthie calls Denver.

She drags me to the Salvation Army store on Colfax, a wide, loud street where cowboys still roam. The store smells of sweat and disaster. I keep to the doorway while Ruthie rummages, then emerges with something muddy colored. Even her underwear comes from there.

Then we eat lemon meringue pie and try on hats at May D & F, Denver's genteel department store. The hats are my idea, big floppy things in white veil or straw. I laugh with her when we look in the mirror together, but secretly love myself in these hats rising and dipping around my face like huge flowers and me the center.

'Can you even imagine wearing this back home?' She turns from the mirror in a hat with a cascade of silk daisies. The brim seems to point to her big nose and firm chin.

She stares at me in my large white veil floppy and her face grows sad. 'You look cute in that.' 'Cute' is not what I want to hear, so I shrug off the compliment. 'Really,' she says.

We've been lured to this shadowless city by fellowships. She's Manhattan, I'm Queens; she lords it over me because Queens is not really the city, but a suburb aching to join the clamour of downtown. Even so, Ruthie has made me her best friend. I must not forget her voice breaking through the hard dry days of my first year here.

But there are secrets she will never know about me. I keep a postcard in my bedroom of a woman drowning in a riverbed of flowers, so peaceful now that she's given up the struggle. Lydia, who shares our office, gave it to me after I admired her print of Chatterton on his deathbed beneath a casement window.

'It calms me just to look at him,' she said. A week later I found Ophelia on my desk. I had to take her home because if Ruthie ever saw, she would say 'how decadent'.

Lydia is one of these graduate student prairie women who wear long dresses and boots and talk about pregnancy dreams. I have never had a pregnancy dream, but in the night my mother stands on the other side of the door pounding. I wake to silence and then I know what Lydia means about the calm. Ophelia, Chatterton. In their dying hearts is the finality I long for.

I have another secret from Ruthie which I will never share with anyone. I am in love with Professor Levine. What shames me is not that he's my advisor or that he's married, or even that he's twice my age and probably shorter than me. How could anyone but the most pathetic fall for a skinny, white-faced man with a pendulous nose and wisps of eyebrows above his Denver blues? That's what I call them for they are relentless. When he sneers at my little ideas and gives me one of his sideways grins, I feel elated, his sarcasm like an embrace. I imagine us in bed together, me caressing his bald head, his arms around me, the two of us like skeletons dancing; for I am, in my mother's words, 'a bony wonder'.

Ruthie makes do with men. She sees John, a big guy with a beard down to his waist who wanders around the department telling everyone he's becoming a Jew. She doesn't mind him using her to gain entrance to the 'land of Canaan' as he calls it, or his stink.

We're on one of our jaunts down Colfax. Ruthie's just bought a black full-length slip she pulled out of one of the boxes of underwear at the Salvation Army. She came right out of the dressing room wearing it in front of all the creepy guys. Just to show me. They took no notice, the downcast ones picking through racks of brown winter jackets. Only the young guy trying on stilettos grinned at her. I'm wondering when Ruthie will wear her slip, since I've never seen her in a dress.

Still, she's feeling good. When I pause in front of a store I haven't noticed before, a tiny place which catches me because in the window is my Ophelia, a full size mannequin dressed in white and covered in flowers, Ruthie agrees to go in even though she's ready for cake.

Inside the tiny dark room a young woman in a floppy straw hat sits at a high counter working on something. She puts whatever it is away and gives us a slow smile full of misshapen teeth. I sniff the air but smell only velvet and the incense the woman is burning near her busy fingers.

Ruthie does a bit of flicking. 'Will you look at the price of this?'

'Are these second hand?' she asks.

'Second or third,' the woman says.

Ruthie whispers to me that this is a resale store where women try to make a profit from fancy dresses they've only worn once. She doesn't want to stay.

I imagine myself in one of the gowns walking into Professor Levine's office, my skin as white as his against black velvet. I shake my head free of this for I have not bought a dress or skirt for years. Skirts come up short and dresses hang on me, wrinkling where they should fit, folds of material over my emptiness. Tears come to my eyes. I will look like a badly clothed scarecrow.

Ruthie sighs. She says she'll wait outside. 'Precious, so precious,' she whispers loud enough for the woman to hear. But I know why she hates it in here. She has to feel like a discoverer in the murk of other people.

I have a session with Professor Levine the next day. For once he does not criticise what I have written, but says something which confuses me. I haven't told Ruthie that I'm working on the final draft of my dissertation and can see the end. She's been stuck for two years on her final chapter. She goes to Levine only to whine.

He's sitting there in an open white shirt, sleeves half rolled up, his legs stretched out. His smile is almost friendly though I take care with what I say for he loves to make fun of me and then turn cold when I too become playful. I was almost late because I dress for him and today I wasn't right in anything. I settled for my boy jeans and black tee shirt, hoping the sight of my pale face with hair tied at the neck will make him think Pre-Raphaelite because I'm certain this is the look he craves: a pale reed woman like the belle dame of his favourite poet. But he doesn't notice me as a woman. I'm just a mind to him, and not a very good one.

Suddenly he's talking about Jane Eyre's quest for transcendence, and I'm thinking that I would have to insert whole sections, bringing the dissertation up from its dungeons of desire. 'But that means changing everything, doesn't it?' He gives me one of his kryptonite looks, eyes fixed on me, thin mouth quivering because he's poised to make one of his sharp little comments which will hurt me, but then in retrospect have a pleasing tenderness, like a healing wound which tickles. He says nothing, only shrugs and indicates our time is over. 'I suppose I could do it,' I say, but he's looking out the window as if I'm already gone.

In the afternoon Ruthie wants to go out for cakes as usual, but I'm aching to get back to the tiny store. I can't have her moaning around me while I try on. I don't want a bargain; I want to spend myself in that store so when I emerge I will be like that figure of glory Professor Levine dreams of.

I go along with Ruthie and then after we part, I circle around the streets of Capital Hill where the flat city rises and falls, and come back to Colfax. Why I must hide my return to this store from her I don't understand. At first I don't find the store and think that maybe it appeared just on that day like *Brigadoon*. Then I see Ophelia and notice for the first time the store's name, written in purple: *Chrysalis*.

The same woman bent over her work looks up. She doesn't remember me. Her pale lashes, the weedy hair sticking out of her hat and her crooked teeth make me feel dizzy. There's something not right about her, as if she has been broken up and re-formed with some of the wrong pieces.

I try on a black kaftan dress, but it swamps me in the little curtained changing room. I put on the green velvet empire waist, but its short tight puffy sleeves make my arms look like spindles. All the other dresses are too short. I sit down on the little stool and hear my mother wonder what a sensible girl like me wants with an old-fashioned floor-length velvet dress. I put on my tee shirt and sneakers, my boy jeans.

The woman watches me hang up the dresses.

'Have you been lucky?' she asks.

I shake my head. 'None of them fit. I'm sorry.' Why should I be sorry? Always.

I turn away and begin pulling open the door when I hear her call out 'wait' in a peculiar hoarse way like a boy whose voice has just broken.

She goes to a back room. It seems a long time before she returns with an armful of crimson velvet and shakes out a dress which makes me hungry. She gives no explanation about why it was in the back. I decide it just arrived, some woman finally deciding to give up.

I come out to stand before the mirror. The long puffy sleeves shield my thin arms. The skirt falls in waves from the fitted low-cut bodice which makes me look full. I turn and turn again trying to see myself from all sides. It is as if the dress were made for me, even to the length. It just touches my heels, its soft velvet like the hands of a fairy godmother.

Back in the changing room I bring the velvet up to my face and sniff. No sweat or stale sadness of Ruthie's Salvation Army, but something else. I sniff again and decide it is the incense the woman burns. Someone has bought this dress and not worn it even once.

The dress costs more than what I spend on a week's food, but I will have it. I will be like those lanky prairie women whose skirts trail over hiking boots. I will come into Professor Levine's office like a vision.

The dress hangs like a woman in a swoon over my arm. She reaches for it. I can't bear to see the velvet slipped into one of these wrinkled paper bags Ruthie comes away with from the Salvation Army, but she folds the dress and carefully wraps a length of purple tissue around it.

Next week I'm in my cubicle, my head down on a pile of freshman papers, when Ruthie gives me a poke. She wants me to come cake eating with her in the afternoon, but I've got Professor Levine at two. It was the only appointment left.

'Again? You saw him a minute ago.'

'You know he's asking for changes.'

She doesn't buy this. 'How many times do you see him?'

'Just once a week.'

'For god's sake Cathy, why d' you see him so much?'

'Maybe it's not once a week.'

She looks at me: 'You're holding something from me?'

'You've been here longer. I'm just getting going.'

We have a strange moment when she keeps trying to get me to look her straight in the eyes, but I don't.

'Stay on the bridge then,' she says, turning her back.

Ruthie is right. I see him too much and the last time he looked at me not with irritation but curiosity: what does she want, this girl? For he is innocent when it comes to sex. I'm sure he has only ever slept with his high-bosomed, haughty wife.

I make up questions for him, questions and questions of questions. He tells me I need to read this one and that one. All the time I'm thinking of the scarlet dress like it is my sad daughter.

So why do I go back to the store again? Ruthie at least wears the clothes she buys. Ophelia is still in the window and incense burns at the grey-eyed woman's side as she does her close work. I turn to the other racks of long dresses, all of flimsy material: silk, organdie, lace. Again I find nothing to fit and again the woman brings out a long dress just waiting for me, of white lacy material like a bride's nightgown. It fits around my body like seaweed. I hear someone, could be Ruthie, could be my mother, cry out when I bring the dress up to the counter and take out my wallet. 'Never,' they cry like a Greek chorus, 'Never will you wear this.'

'It's amazing,' I say to grey eyes, 'It fits me to a T.'

She smiles at me, blinking her long colorless lashes.

It's a mistake to meet Ruthie after that with the purple tissue paper bundle in my arms. She's so nosy. But I couldn't keep saying no to her. Even though her pronouncements on everyone else drives them away, she's my only real friend out here, the one who when I'm shaking with flu, will come with her own spoon and cough medicine.

She's standing outside the Salvation Army with one of their wrinkled bags.

'What'd you get?' I ask.

'What'd you get?' Already she's torn the tissue paper.

'Hey.' I grab it back and hold it close to my chest.

'You've been there again, haven't you? You realise what a rip-off they are? Used clothing they're selling like new.'

'They're antique,' I say.

She pulls out of her bag a long burgundy dress with embroidery across the front, the ethnic kind which just hangs and you know no one in India or Istanbul would ever wear it. She's still pulling stuff out: a satiny blouse which feels synthetic, a black blazer with padded shoulders. I don't say that I can see the shine on one of the sleeves.

'You had a success,' I say.

'All this for ten dollars. How much did that cost you?'

'So good for you.'

'Tell me.' She pulls at the tissue paper and manages to rip it so the dress is exposed in all it laciness.

'What is with you?'

'Should we try on hats? Or do you want to eat something?'

'I wanna know what you're buying this for.'

I think for a moment that she suspects about Professor Levine, and blush to think of myself in love with the man of bone.

'I'm going to a wedding.'

She takes this in then says: 'You're wearing white to a wedding?'

'Oh. I forgot.'

Ruthie hunches up one shoulder and turns from me. I take her arm. 'C'mon Ruthie. Let's eat cake.'

'Don't bullshit me, Cathy. Ever.'

I calm her at May D & F talking about her favorite subject, the prairie women.

'Don't you go becoming like them,' she says.

'What do you mean?'

'Just don't get all vague. Like Lydia.'

She looks at me almost tenderly and I see she worries about losing me, me more than grey beard John.

We share a slice of seven-layer cake and go off to the hat department. The floppys of summer have gone. We're trying on fur hats and berets. Ruthie scoops up her long hair and tucks it all into a black beret, then turns to me. I am hoping she doesn't notice the shock on my face. I'm looking not at her, but Professor Levine: the same long white face, big nose, even the eyes. I don't say anything, of course I don't say anything. She keeps looking at herself in the mirror and laughing. I'm sick with looking at her, reach over and pull at the beret till her brown mane straggles down her long neck.

'Hey.' She turns from the mirror. 'Why'd you do that, I was having fun.'

'You looked like a jerk.'

I sit at my desk in my shoebox bedroom, my hands in folds of scarlet velvet. I feel a wild joy every time I put it on. Sometimes I fear such joy as if the dress will flame up and consume me. Yesterday it was the turn of the wedding dress as I typed. Still perfumed not with incense I've decided, but some musk enduring even after I have washed it.

'Something's going on.' Ruthie talks while she eats her coconut custard pie. She's seen Lydia go into Professor Levine's office and emerge hours later.

'How do you know? She could've come and gone and then gone back again. You didn't hang around there.'

'I did actually.'

'But he…' I do that funny thing where my throat ends up in my mouth and I have to swallow before I can speak.

'Yeah, I know, he's pure. But what's she doing?'

'Talking. She told me she's run into a block.'

'Her head maybe.'

I watch her spoon the remains of the coconut custard pie into her mouth and think of Lydia's moon face rising above the flat land. You could never know these prairie women. Maybe Lydia had loves as strange as her Chatterton.

I can't sit still anymore.

'What about your éclair?'

We both look at the long lean pastry. Ruthie begins to laugh.

'I'm going home.'

'So go. I'm fed up with hats anyway.'

But I walk to my store. I rummage around, then stand before the young woman about to say what I always say. She's hard at work, head bent, so very occupied that she does not notice me. I look down to see her long fingers pasting silver sequins on an eggshell. She's nearly finished one side and the egg lies there like a fallen moon. I am open mouthed at this so say nothing for some minutes. A shifting of my feet alerts her and she covers the egg with a length of watery silk.

'Have you been lucky?' She asks.

'No not this time. But maybe you have something else.'

At this point she will bring out something, I know she will. But she shakes her head.

'She hasn't come in. Not this week. Not last.'

I stare at her, her grey eyes and wispy hair. Ruthie was right. She was not born a woman.

'You mean they're all from one person? Well I figured. They both fit so perfectly.' Only I hadn't. Nobody had ever owned the dresses before me, and even I could not possess them.

'The only problem with them is the smell. Not a bad smell, but I can't get rid of it.'

She looks at me sadly.

Maybe she's died, the woman who has given me her velvet and lace. 'Has she, I mean do you think?' I choke even though I'm smiling, so the sentence never finishes. I'm wearing ghost's clothes, smelling her sweetness from the grave.

It's then I smell the perfume again and realise it comes from her. For once she's not burning incense and I can smell her or him or whoever.

'She doesn't come,' she repeats.

I can see she longs to get back to her eggshell.

That night I dream again about my mother. We're in our yard. She tells me to get the apple from the very top of the tree. Only that one will do. I climb for hours, pushing myself through dense branches which tear at my face. When I'm clear, I reach for the apple, but close my hand on a cloud, a seed flower.

My next appointment with Professor Levine is Friday. In those days before, I keep to my apartment. I don't even show up for my office hour with my freshman students on Wednesday. Because I don't want to meet Lydia, see her dresses trailing into Levine's office, moon-face Lydia, Ophelia of the prairie.

On Friday morning I'm in my jeans and black shirt typing at the little desk. I'm supposed to see him at eleven. At least I know that Lydia won't be there before me. She writes at night, then sleeps until lunch, like some wraith, some sister of Dracula.

I smell again the perfume and am drawn to my dresses. The white lace clings as nothing has ever done before. As I let my hair down I see myself lying face upwards in a lake, Professor Levine reaching into the wet leaves for me.

I know I will be back in my jeans again before I leave, and the bride dress will wait for me with its smell of the boy woman. 'Sometimes a dress finds you,' she said when I bought the last one. I whisper her words to myself.

I'm pulling on my boots, going out the door with my books in my arms because I couldn't wear a knapsack with the dress. The boots yes, Lydia would wear them with a ball gown, but never the knapsack. She carries her books in beaded bags which hang from her flat arms.

All the way down Capital Hill to Broadway I know I'll go home. I could call the department secretary to say I'm too sick to see him. Even on the bus, crossing my legs in the stretchy lace, I know I won't see him like this. But the dress carries me above even the plateau on which the city rests, for I have lost the substance of myself, my bones filled with light.

I'm walking up to my office, lifting my dress as I mount each step. When I look inside the room I share with four others, I see no one. I creep to my cubicle to wait. Then I hear steps and see a long braid of hair. If I slump down she might not see me, for her cubicle is at the other end of the room.

But I know she will come looking. As I hear her moving towards me, I fold my arms over my chest and look down at some student papers.

Ruthie starts to speak then stops. 'What are you?'

I will her not to laugh at me, but she does not even smile. 'I'm late,' I say, though I have minutes.

She continues to stare at me. Something has happened to her mouth because it doesn't speak. Then she asks, 'Late for who? Just who?'

'Who do you think?'

'You're seeing him in that?'

I look down at myself.

'You're having a thing with him.'

'Are you kidding?'

'Tell me. I wanna know. I need to know.' Her lips are actually trembling.

'Why should I? With him?' I start to say 'he's so ugly', but I can't.

She looks angry. Maybe she knows how much she resembles Levine. 'You are. I know you are. I can see right through you.'

The lacy material hides nothing. Not even my nipples.

'Why didn't you tell me? You could have. You don't really care for him.'

I raise both my hands high to plead my innocence and feel the thin material tear. 'Shit.'

'All along I thought he was pure and that's why I never really tried, though I wanted to. So much. Just offer myself.'

Is it shock or something else making me dizzy? I regain myself and look at her sad face.

'That's why I avoided him. It was breaking my heart.'

'Ruthie, I never. Believe me.'

She sits down and puts her hands over her face.

I put my arm around her. 'I thought I was the only one. But believe me, he never.'

She wipes her eyes and nose and gives me one of her looks which almost relieves me for it is Ruthie I see again.

'Are you kidding? There's not one woman in the department who doesn't want him. Just to have him sneer at you. It's unbearable.' She wipes her eyes. 'You got a tissue?'

I shake my head.

'So gimme something.' She points to my pad of notes. I tear out the first page. 'Hey that has writing on it,' she says.

I shrug. 'Go on. I don't need it.' It's a page of questions I was planning to ask him carefully formed so that he could not look beneath the words and see me. I watch her blow her nose in it.

'You're really not?' She stares hard into my face. 'So why the fuck are you dressed for it?'

To this I say nothing. I smell again the sharp sweetness like a scent of madness. I want to rip off what little I have on.

We hear laughter from the direction of his office. The moon face of Lydia passes through the doorway beyond our cubicles.

Ruthie just stares, then she whispers, 'Her.'

She'll fill him with her emptiness.

'Can I wear your jacket? Just to go in there?'

'Fool,' Ruthie says, but she gives it to me, the one with the padded shoulders and second hand shine. With the jacket buttoned up, he'll see only a skirt of lace.

'Wish me luck.' Why did I say that? I can't tell her I'm handing in my last chapter.

She gives me one of her Manhattan up and down stares. 'You look like a jerk.'

I just stand there waiting.

'So good luck already. You want me to spit on you like my grandmother does?'

As I turn I hear her whisper so low that I don't know if she's speaking to me or herself, 'I'll miss you.'

I'm in there talking to his silence. There's something naked about his face; the eyes once so fearsome seem mere lights. I hand him the pages I typed in my scarlet dress, in my lace.

'I worked transcendence into it,' I say.

He smiles but not at me, and I think how many times I've cradled that death's head.

I'm circling around Colfax. Not returning, not ever, but when I shut my eyes the boy woman holds out a dress cut from the Denver sky.

In the window of the *Chrysalis*, Ophelia has fallen from her bed and lost all her flowers. She's not a mannequin after all, but a big doll whose lashed eyes have opened. Words shape themselves in the hollow of her mouth. 'She comes again,' I hear her say.

And I make for home.

Waiting in the Darkness

Sally Flint

The smell of burnt toast, stale urine and gangrenous flesh hit my nostrils. 'Morning George, morning Henry, morning all.' I had perfected a walk that told patients this nurse is in a hurry, she's got something important to do, don't interrupt her with your aches, your moans about cold tea or toilet needs. I slipped between the curtains drawn around Percy's bed.

'Morning.'

The doctor was standing over Percy, his white coat creased and spattered with drops of antiseptic.

'Ah Staff Nurse – we carried on without you.' He placed a clear plastic container with a screw top lid into the palm of my hand. 'Take these to the office will you. I'll be along to sort out the paper work.'

The contents of the jar felt warm. Percy's foot was sticking out from beneath the sheet, a shade of purple. His drip was not dripping. 'I didn't realise.'

'About an hour ago.'

'I see.'

'I've packed the sockets; now some discreet needlework. Don't want to upset the relatives.'

I absorbed the scene; Percy no longer breathing; the doctor with his open suture pack about to start probing at loose flesh, and the container. In it were two pinkish white orbs sprinkled with lines of red and yellow mucous. They weighed more than ping pong balls, less than golf balls; the meaty weight of gristle or muscle. At the centre of each ball was a circle of blue. Percy's eyeballs, still watching, here in my hand.

I wanted to drop them and run back past the living, past the office, down the stairs, out to space and fresh air. The contents of the specimen jar were still watching me. I transferred my grip and held the container by the silver screw top. What if the screw top was loose – what if I let go – what if these two little globes put into my care fell to the floor? I imagined crawling under beds and wheeling back lockers as the two errant balls collected fluff and stickiness across the ward vinyl.

'Alright?' The doctor asked, but remained absorbed in his embroidery.

'I'll put them in the office. On the desk. Ready for you,' I said in my unaffected voice; the voice I saved for traumas of blood and gore. I left the container on the desk and continued to the staff toilet where I threw up, glad I hadn't had time for breakfast.

'You alright love?' Myra the ward cleaner bellowed over the door. I came out and splashed my hands and face. 'There are only two reasons why a nurse is sick in the morning.'

'I'm not pregnant and I'm not hung-over.' I replied.

'Well someone had better get on with breakfasts. I heard about Percy, went in the night, thought he'd be a lingerer. If I was in that state, I've told my family…'

'Remember, Bill is nil by mouth, George is high fibre, Charlie is diabetic even though he'll beg you for sugar and Mick is spoons only.'

'Spoons only?' Myra questioned.

'If you'd lost both legs to gangrene, your wife and your job, could you be trusted with a knife?' I couldn't help but look at my own reflection. Just how tricky was it to scoop eyeballs from their sockets and manoeuvre them into a tiny plastic pot?

'Poor old Percy,' said Nancy coming down the ward with the linen trolley.

'It's for the best,' I said.

'Yes, well Sister wants us to do the honours.'

'Can't you get one of the students to help you lay him out?'

'What students? There's only one this morning and she's bathing and making beds and getting Bill ready for theatre.' She looked at me, suddenly concerned. 'You okay?'

'I didn't get much sleep last night, but I've got tomorrow off,' I said.

'You're so pale. Do you want me to do the drug round?'

'We'll do it together. It'll be quicker. Then we'll do Percy.'

*

Percy had taken on a darker blue around his extremities.

'You'd have thought the night staff would have put his teeth in.' Nancy sighed.

'I'll wash his face.' I was careful to avoid the tiny black dots of thread around his lids.

'Terrible to see such a nice man suffer. I thought he'd last another week at least.' Nancy removed the catheter.

'Mind the…' There was the spurt of blood, still red, still liquid in his veins.

'Someone's on the phone from the bed management team.' The student nurse poked round the screen and I watched her colour drain.

'Nancy, can you tell them we haven't any empty beds. Nurse Carter can help here. It'll be good experience.'

I gave the student the job of clearing the contents of Percy's locker while I got on with straightening his legs, his arms, each finger and thumb. 'Sometimes a patient can be dead for several hours and still let out a breath. Just warning you; it's air left in the lungs.'

The student looked on wide-eyed.

'No need to be scared. Touch him. Percy wouldn't mind.' I knew the coldness of his flesh would shock her. I pulled up his pyjama jacket. 'The knack is to get it over the head first. Rigor mortis starts setting in after an hour. It begins in the neck and jaw muscles, proceeds to the chest and upper extremities, finally reaching the lower limbs. It can last a few minutes or several days. Now comb his hair and on with the gown.'

'Doesn't it upset you?' the student asked.

'When they've collected the body, you can wipe down the locker and bed.'

I removed the dressings from the pressure sores, repacked them with ribbon gauze and sealed them with substantial amounts of Micropore tape. I stroked Percy's arm where the drip had left a bruise and squeezed his hand one last time - then removed the chrysanthemums from the vase on his locker and deposited them in the bin.

'Come on quick,' Nancy called me to the empty side ward. 'I've pinched something off the trolley.'

We stood there chewing rubber toast and gulping tea. 'My legs still ache from last night,' I moaned. 'I didn't get away 'til well after ten. Nancy, I was hoping to disappear early today if you'll cover the last bit of the shift.'

'Yeah, that's fine by me.' Nancy was scratching – the alcohol rub made her hands really raw. 'Forgot to say we've a new patient after lunch – can't remember his name, a TIA – and Pharmacy phoned too; they're coming to check stocks tomorrow morning.'

'What? But they're not due for another fortnight. I'm not in tomorrow. I'll never get off early now.'

'I've covered before on your day off.'

Outside the window, the porters were wheeling the mortuary trolley across the car park.

Nancy continued talking with her mouth full. 'You know Percy's wife begged me to help him last weekend. She said you wouldn't let an animal…'

'Better get back on the ward – we'll talk later.' I left Nancy and met the porters at the lift.

'One for Rose Cottage?' called Bob.

I nodded.

'What about it then nurse?'

'What about what?'

'You know you can't resist me.'

'Shut up, Bob.' I pointed at my wedding ring.

'Well I don't mind if you don't.'

'Enough. And it would be good if you could get a trolley that didn't squeak. We can hear you…'

'Coming?' He grinned.

'Shut up.'

'Hope this one's tagged and bagged right,' muttered the porter with the tinted glasses.

'He's ready to go.'

'Brakes on.' They lifted Percy with ease from his mattress. 'Come on old boy.'

I went to the office and started writing the report, relieved Percy's eyeballs had gone. There stood Ada. I didn't want her thanks and she didn't want my sympathy, but convention told us otherwise. 'I'm so sorry Ada.' I recalled our conversation from the previous evening; how she had cried. 'He's at rest now,' I told her.

Ada sat on the edge of the chair gripping the sides.

'I want to say thank...'

'There's no need.' I interrupted her mid sentence.

'You know about the organ donation?' Her voice was just audible.

'Yes, that was...' I was floundering for the right words. Percy's eyes would be staring from a fridge shelf within the confines of the morgue.

'He was a generous man. Even at the end he was a...' The tears came and I pulled a Kleenex from the box kept on the desk. 'It would have been our Golden Wedding Anniversary next week.'

'I know; he told me,' I lied.

Ada half smiled. 'He's never forgotten our anniversary.'

'You seemed such a devoted couple, so many memories.'

'Yes – memories. You must see so much.'

As I wished for something to interrupt us, the door opened.

'I've done Percy's belongings.' The student nurse stood in the doorway with two plastic bags. Stupid, insensitive girl I thought, and then wondered if I had ever made the same error of judgement. I placed the bags at Ada's side knowing the contents. An apple (soft), an orange (hard), a half finished crossword book, a biro, dressing gown, pyjamas (clean), pyjamas (dirty), a watch, a razor, half a bottle of squash, towel, face cloth (damp), comb, slippers (nearly new), and a pair of spectacles.

I watched Ada take her arthritic limbs and the two carrier bags slowly across the car park. Another widow who didn't want to go home, but I supposed she would soon be reunited with her husband.

We straightened pillows, soothed anxieties and gave medicine. We joked and commented on the weather. We didn't stop.

'Myra, can you sort out the dinner trolley please?'

'Eye, eye,' she said and saluted.

Nancy and I hid in the large cupboard off the kitchen and scoffed some mash and steamed fish that Myra had saved back for us.

'And I want to check with you on something – about last night,' Nancy whispered.

'There's someone coming,' Myra screeched through the crack in the door. We both ditched our plates and sidled onto the ward. The Nursing Officer patrolled the hospital at mealtimes like a bloated fish.

'I've seen her watch as a whole tray of liver and onions has been emptied into the pig bin,' whispered Nancy. 'Frog face.'

As the Nursing Officer walked towards me, I could count her chins and see my reflection in her bulbous eyes. How easy it would be to just lean her forward and tap her on the back of the head – voilà – eyes ready for the taking. Percy's eyes had been deep set; they must have clung to their cavities. Thank goodness just the corneas were used in transplants - otherwise someone could end up unbalanced with one protuding eye.

'You are aware that it is instant dismissal if staff are caught eating the patients' food. Are you listening Staff Nurse?' I nodded, but stood well back in case she caught the smell of haddock on my breath. 'And pray, why is that bed still unmade when it is past lunch time?'

'The patient has recently been transferred to Rose Cottage.'

'That's no excuse. I'm not happy with things on this ward. I'll be back.'

'Oh jolly good,' I wanted to yell in her amphibian face. 'You narrow-minded, never-had-a-man-in-your-life spinster, never held two eyeballs in your hand at seven thirty in the morning.'

'Where's that student nurse? Tell her to get that bed made up and I'd better do Mick's dressings,' I shouted at Nancy.

'Think the gangrene is still spreading?' Nancy asked.

'What do you think?' I snapped. 'And when you've done that explain to Bill, the intricacies of a cholecystectomy. See if he wants to keep his gall stones as a souvenir.'

'Staff Nurse, you can do the report this afternoon. It's good experience for you.'

'Yes Sister.' I talked through each individual patient, their conditions, their prognosis, their treatment and started to delegate work to the other nurses who had arrived for the late shift.

The phone rang and Sister answered it. She held her hand over the receiver and said, 'Staff nurse, there's to be an autopsy.'

I swallowed hard and didn't question the Sister who never smiled. 'On the patient who died.'

'Percy? But we know the cause of death was carcinoma of the ...'

'They want someone from the ward to attend.' She removed her hand from the receiver. 'Our Staff Nurse will be with you shortly.'

I had no wish to see Percy's innards removed, dissected and taken for analysis. I had no fascination to see the way the carcinomas had invaded his cavities. I could do without the noise of drilling filling my head and knowing the weight of his heart, liver and brain. I had no desire to see the cause of his death questioned. She saw me shudder and took pleasure in saying, 'In half an hour then Staff Nurse.'

*

The smell of the mortuary clung. At home I put my uniform on a hot wash, locked the bathroom door and turned on the taps. The water's warmth unpacked my emotions, made me drowsy. I saw strange things. Drip needles curled like snakes waiting to strike; Ada, a handful of pebbles to her mouth; I saw Percy staring at me.

I was relieved to hear footsteps on the stairs. He tried the door then knocked. 'Alright in there? Glass of wine?'

'Already got one. I won't be a minute.' Naked, I watched the water disappear down the drain then wrapped my body in soft towelling. I joined my husband on the landing and kissed him, glad to touch his warmth.

'How was work?' he asked.

'Busy,' I replied.

'What's for tea?' he said.

'Oh yes, I've really had time to shop and cook.'

'Don't snap at me. You're not the only one who's been at work all day.'

'Lets eat out.' I emptied the bottle of wine into my glass.

'You don't look in a fit state.' He took the glass of wine off me.

'How would you know? I'm tired that's all.' I took back the glass, swapping it for the empty bottle. I screwed up my face, stuck out my tongue and grinned.

'I don't know how you get away with it.'

'With what?'

'I suppose you're back on duty at the crack of dawn.'

'Actually I've got a whole day off tomorrow.'

'Yeah right 'til you get a call they're short staffed. I'll get a take-way,' he said.

'Adrian,' I beckoned him towards me.

'What now?'

'I don't want to get old.'

'You won't.' He shook his head. 'I see you had time to stop and buy more wine.'

*

The smell of burnt toast and stale urine met me on the stairs. Nancy stood at the top. 'Mick's gone then.'

'Just after we went off duty yesterday. He was in a terrible state.'

'Yes. How come I've been called in on my day off?' I ran up the last four steps before I realised Nancy had been crying.

'Come on, pull yourself together Nancy. Go and get yourself a coffee, I'll cover for you.'

'No, I can't. We're both wanted in the office. The Head of Pharmacy says he wants to question everybody.'

'You've nothing to worry about,' I muttered. 'Go to the canteen and don't come back for half an hour.'

Nancy was a good nurse, but she cried too easily. I smoothed my uniform and walked into the office. I thought of blind Percy, waiting in the darkness, his eyelids sewn together.

Around us, the Dark

Liz Gifford

It was two weeks after her mother's funeral. They gave her back her summer job at the telephone exchange. So, on the night of the Lynmouth disaster she was there, trying to put people through as the river rose up in the darkness and plucked the houses away from the village. At the end of the night shift the girls stood in a group, crying. But, Patricia didn't want that. She pushed her bike home through the moist darkness, her arms trembling.

She kept thinking that she was the last person to hear some of those voices before the flood carried them away into oblivion.

The house was in darkness when she got back. She went upstairs and stood outside Queenie's door, hoping for some feeling of company. Queenie lay thrown across the bed covers, still in all her clothes.

Down in the kitchen, she turned on the light. She put a match to the stove and stood next to the blue flame, feeling its small heat. Her mother's drab pinny was still hanging on a nail, the pink and grey flowers washed and washed to shadows. There was a pile of condolence cards on the edge of the dresser, each one bordered in thick black ink, commiserating with the girls for their loss. Two weeks' dust on the dresser and the cards.

She picked up the kettle to fill it. The lino made a tacky sound as she moved, pulling at her shoe. She should mop the floor; that was what you were supposed to do.

A quick flash of anger, because what she was supposed to be doing was sitting in the library in London, studying her Latin poetry; untangling pentameters to see the shape of a tall figure as he walked up from the sea. How the girl on the shore looked up and suddenly saw his comely shape outlined against the water, saw that she would love him.

She heard the creak of footsteps coming down the stairs. Queenie came in.

'He was there again Pat, down in the street. He stopped and looked up for ages.'

'Don't be so soft. You're imagining it.'

'He knows we're on our own.'

'How does he know that, unless he knows us? Makes no sense. Now get you to bed, and this time, get in your nightdress.'

'Pat.'

'What?'

'Your accent's come back. You don't talk so London now. I like that.'

'I told you Queenie, I'm not Pat now. I'm Patricia.'

'You won't go back, will you?'

Silence, then, 'I won't go back.'

She pushed the back door bolt in place, checked the front door was locked, all the windows firmly shut. She lay listening to the dark for a long time. But as soon as she slept, the front door was standing wide open again to the water-sheened night, the thick dark coming in like wet breath.

She woke, her heart pounding, could feel the damp air coming in from her dream. Then she had to go down to check the door was really locked, aware of her own black form moving through the shadows.

In the morning the sky was dense and white across the window; she had to make herself get up. The clothes on the back of her chair hung heavy, as if the night dew had soaked into them as she slept.

'Pat, I bain't got no clean under things left.'

'Well you got to get and wash them then,' she said, in that final way that mum had, hard at the edges, shifting and molten with old grief inside.

'Look what I found,' said Queenie. 'In mum's bag.'

It was that old letter from dad, the last one, folded round a brown photo of two small girls, their faces cracked from being drowned in his pocket all over Christmas week. Waiting for him never to come home. His last letter.

'Someone's got to get the shopping.' She was still in her slip. She pulled on a dress.

Outside, she put mum's wicker basket on one handle of the bike. Along the high street, the news sellers' placards were out on the pavement. Messages written in black about the Lynmouth disaster. People standing around to read them. She thought about her mother's grave stone and the rain in the churchyard; the rain that carried on till the river Lynn broke.

In the covered market she looked for cheap things. The stewing end of mutton, pearl barley to make it go further. She had mum's long purse, both their ration cards.

Outside the row of butcher shops were chairs with their huge bowls of clotted cream, crusted with buttery yellow on the top. She knew that taste, sweet, unguent and healing as ointment, but she hadn't got the ration points. Suddenly, she was empty and poor, envious of a younger self, holding on to dad's hand as he said yes, get some cream to their mum, and the butcher ladled it up. To have on blackberry pie, like eating summer with cream on it.

She waited in the queue, the wet, rusty smell of the butcher's sawdust and blood around her.

The woman in front of her had pale cotton gloves. 'Three dozen people gone at Lynmouth then,' she said.

Patricia put the scrag-end in the basket and, walking out, almost collided with him. He was there in front of her in his long, tweed coat, grey hairs in his nostrils.

'Ain't you coming to see us then? Mary's in there.'

Against her will, she was back in the narrow haberdasher's shop, Mary, his wife, yellow, sour and ill behind the counter. The same close smell, faint odours of camphor and formaldehyde from the rolls of cloth. And she was that schoolgirl again, serving in the shop in her grammar school uniform so Mary could cook his tea. Mum so pleased to have the money. The narrow passages behind the desk where he pressed close and hard, because she'd given in once, and then she was trapped. Whispering hot and sour down her neck, 'You won't get no other job if I tell. I know what you're like, don't I? But then, a girl like you, always thinks too much of herself, see.'

She had to get out in the air again. He was pressing a bag into her hand. 'It fits,' he said. 'And she bain't got long to live now. You'll never get enough at that exchange to keep the house.'

'I knows it was you outside our house. You keep away.'

But he laughed.

On the bridge she stopped and when no one could see, ripped the paper open. A nightdress, in slippery rayon, an ugly, beige colour. She was standing on the bridge, the one in the poem that won the prize at school and got her the scholarship to London. It was about the places you leave behind. She was standing on the bridge and she was holding the nightdress, like a sheath of old skin. She held it away and she thought of the restfulness of oblivion, under the cool water.

She let the cellophane package slip from her hands, watched it track through the air, suddenly taken and tossed by the water. The roar in her ears.

The wicker basket cut into her bare forearm as she waited for Queenie to pull back the bolt on the back door.

'I wasn't afeared,' she said, 'but you was a long time gone. What we 'aving for our tea then?'

'How should I know?' snapped Pat, slipping mum's apron over her head. 'You could have at least washed the potatoes.'

She ran the water hard into an enamel bowl in the sink, the crackle of the metal vibrating. The branny earth rose like a scum and she swilled them round.

'Leopold Bloom always carried a potato,' she said.

'Is he your boyfriend in London then?'

She thought of her yellow dress and how she'd danced with a boy once, as if something was beginning.

'Ain't got no boyfriend.'

'Your accent's come back proper,' Queenie said. 'Oh you ain't bought scrag again 'ave you? It don't cook.'

'Scrag is cheap,' shouted Pat. 'So just you shut up.'

And she thought, 'I sound like mum.' The back straps of mum's apron moving as she kneaded the bread dough, shouting, 'to get up them stairs.' The girls reluctant to leave the crackle of the coal fire, Queenie feeding in kindling sticks. Mum coming out, incandescent, a slap across Pat's face, and Queenie, everyone's little blonde songster, already running.

Dad just a letter now. Nothing to help mum. Walking home in the blackout, he'd stepped off the edge of the dock into the dark water.

She'd thought, 'When the time comes, mum and me, we'll make up.' There'd be an understanding. Something completed. Then it was too late.

She'd spent far too much of her scholarship money on a yellow satin dress. Yards and yards of material. She was waiting at the edge of the room and he'd asked her did she like to dance? One arm round her waist, one arm leading her through the music, an odd feeling, as if she recognised him. His hair was not washed under the brilliantine, the effortful self care of growing up in the war, the missing fathers, the missing mothers.

He walked her back to her lodgings, past the bomb sites. He found a patch of anemones growing among the scraped up rubble mounds. 'This was a garden once,' he said. He picked her a bunch of the deep red and purple flowers, the sooty pollen shedding from their centres.

Then she was on the train home. She and Queenie cycling up the hill, feeling her calves would burst, but even so, they still got to the hospital too late.

Supper was finished. Her feet were sticking to the lino around the cooker again. Tack, tack, tack as she carried the pans to the sink, Queenie rolling a pen across the table, her head on her arm. The condolence cards waiting to be answered. 'We should get and clean this bloody house,' she shouted.

It was starting to go dark, but she got out the mops and the rags, swilling water around the floor, clashing the bucket round the kitchen. Loud knocks ricocheting down the stairs as she went at them with a hand brush. Hammering the broom along the hallway, hitting all the walls. Made Queenie strip their beds and fill the copper. They threw the rugs over the washing line to beat at them, and she noticed how it had gone dark. They had to set the whites to boil in clouds of wet steam, washing until past midnight. And still she would not let them go to bed. Vim and the sting of bleach as they scrubbed down the bath, the lavatory. Scouring the cooker with sugar soap, their hands bright red and sore now, moving every pot in the cupboards. Hanging out the white sheets to flap in the dark. Polishing the black windows against the night with balls of newspaper. When it was starting to get light, she said they could go to bed.

The heat of a late summer morning woke her. She was still in her clothes, on the top of the eiderdown.

Queenie came in, her blonde hair pushed up on one side, a funny grey look to her skin.

'We'll go for a swim,' Pat told her, suddenly sorry. 'Like we used to.'

They took the bikes down to Braunton sands, late in the afternoon now. Miles along the lanes, past the cottages with the wood smoke caught in the apple trees. Everything far away, feeling remote as they wheeled past through the air.

Through the acres of dunes, the green peaks like waves of hills at first then resolving into sand. They came to the wide beach, stretching away for miles, the immense flat sea, the silver light mercurial over the grey surface. White salt waves foaming and then running back, dissolving over the hard, bright water. There was no one else in sight.

They undressed. Put on their costumes under towels, ran down to the sea. She tipped up in the water and let the salt sea go in and out of her mouth. The water was cold, but she couldn't register it; she knew it, but couldn't feel it.

As they towelled their cold limbs dry, Queenie said, 'I could Pat, I could go and live with Mrs Wells. And you could go back.'

'But you'd be by yourself then.' If she wasn't looking after Queenie, what was she now?

They rode home without speaking. Pat floating away from herself, watching how she rode through the tiredness, her body numb and exhausted. Queenie whimpering to keep up.

They ate bread with a heel of stale cheddar that had broken out into a sweat. Chewing in silence. The day almost gone now, Queenie's face shadowy. No one bothered to put the light on.

A sudden burst of gunfire, someone knocking hard on the front door. They sat and waited. It made them jump when it started up again. They crept out into the hallway, standing back in the shadows. The top of his head moving away and then coming back close in the glass. But he was knocking again, urgent, insistent, the glass in the door rattling. On and on. He'd have all the neighbours out. Her heart beating fast and sickly, she unlocked the door.

His familiar outline against the street light. Smelling of evening air. A sudden shock like a punch.

'Patricia?' he said. 'I'm sorry, I don't know why, I panicked and I had to make you open the door. I didn't know if something had…you remember me, don't you?'

She stared at him, her face white. She took a step back, and then she was sitting on the bottom step holding onto the banisters, looking up at him, sobbing. 'It's you,' she said.

He was standing with the door open, the street light behind outlining his shape.

And that was what she remembered. That was what she always said to Queenie later, how all the future had come flooding in with him, through the open door.

The Method

Tom J Vowler

I'd read about those actors, the purists who immersed themselves in roles for months, sometimes years, collecting all the experiences, the essence of characters in order to portray them better. If they wanted insight into how being the middleweight champion of the world felt, they'd seek it in the ring from the end of someone's fists.

My own approach to research had never been this committed; if I wanted to write about something, I'd read about it. I'd Google the hell out of it and then use my imagination to make notes and diagrams, charts with lines linking characters, the complex worlds they occupied, their beliefs, histories, idiosyncrasies, what I thought they ate, how they voted. I'd construct their lives, give them voices, breathe life into them. I thought that was enough. But then, at a meeting with my publisher, the issue of authenticity arose.

'I'm not sure we believe in Will,' said Gillian.

'In what way do you not believe in him?'

'He doesn't seem...organic.'

'He's not a root vegetable.'

'The voice slips at times and I'm not really sure what he's feeling when he, you know...'

'Sleeps with large women?'

'Yes. Why do they need to be so big?'

'It's a childhood thing.'

'And the drug-taking sections...they sound contrived.'

'What do you suggest?'

'We like the novel per se. Joff was raving about its filmic potential...'

'I'm not really...'

'We do need to airbrush this…what's he called?'

'Will.'

'Yes. He doesn't resonate. Parts of him feel made up.'

'They are.'

'Yes, yes of course. It doesn't feel as if you know him well enough. Is he essential?'

'To what?

'The story.'

'It's called *Will's Island.*'

'Yes, I wanted to talk to you about the title.'

Once home I got out my notes on Will. Five-eight, early forties, loss adjuster turned journalist turned would-be novelist. I conjured the image of him into my mind, walked around my office talking like him – actual lines of dialogue from the early chapters. I sat down and sketched his face, pinning it above my monitor next to the list of onomatopoeic verbs I made one grey Tuesday afternoon. I began a conversation with him in the mirror, introduced him to Rapunzel, whom he meets in Chapter Fourteen anyway before her violent end sixteen pages later. I liked him.

I e-mailed Gillian: WILL STAYS.

*

As Will had done, I typed 'dating large women' into Google, and as Will did, I signed up for three of the sites. I looked at some profiles but none of their creators looked big enough. Will's thing, you see, is losing himself, almost literally, in women. Their arms and legs, their breasts, have to engulf him. He lets them crush him as though he were a written-off car.

Elaine, 37, from Bath looked the largest of them, so I emailed her. Two weeks and three dates later I was beneath her lolling stomach as it slapped hard onto mine like a trawler landing its catch.

'Can you just lie on me, really still?' I said, which is what he gets them to do.

'Oh, Will,' she moaned.

Diane, 39, from Exeter, had bigger thighs and arms, but said I wasn't her type. I told her she wasn't mine either and that it didn't matter. She didn't finish her drink. A couple more objected to me talking into my dictaphone as they came. Furthermore, none of them matched for mass those I'd described in the latter chapters. There were sites dedicated to bigger women, but their purpose was merely two-dimensional; there was no scope to meet them. Others implied a financial exchange, but as Will doesn't do this, I was reluctant to. Instead I considered the relativity of size.

In the meantime, I turned my mind to other parts of his life. Will had worked on a national but I had to start somewhere. The editor at the *Herald* explained that their trainee journalists were usually straight from college, an English or media degree behind them, some post-grad study to boot. But he'd heard of one of my novels – the one they dramatised badly – and said to go in for a chat.

'Bit late for a career move, isn't it?'

'I think reporting's in my bones.'

'Might be a bit dry for you: council meetings, petty crime…'

'Dry's good.'

'Send some articles in and we'll see.'

My largely embellished CV meant I had to learn quickly. Sleeping three or four hours a night, I studied contempt of court and local authorities and was up to seventy words a minute shorthand in a fortnight. I spent two whole days in the library reading every piece in every *Herald* from the last five years. There was such a depressingly formulaic structure that I wondered how Will had coped with it. Three weeks after meeting the editor, I walked around the town interviewing its dreary cohorts as they went about their newsworthy business. I sent in three disparate stories and a week later I was a trainee journalist on twelve grand.

*

If I couldn't make the women bigger…

Calories became my nemesis; I could tell you how many were found in almost any food. I cut down to six hundred a day, then four hundred. I jogged to and from work and used the paper's gym in my 'lunch' hour. I hadn't exercised since my twenties and my body let me know it. Initially, the changing room was the only place I drew attention.

'Shit, mate. You lose any more weight, you'll be able to fax yourself to work.'

I got breakfast down to an apple. Lunch was a banana, dinner a tin of tuna.

I grew a beard; reading my notes and the early chapters again, I found no reference to Will's, beyond that he had one. His clothes were easier to mimic, though I needed ever smaller ones.

Now there was less of me, I joined some more sites.

'Shit,' said Caroline, 42, from Clevedon, as I took off my shirt. 'Your spine, I can see all along it.'

I told her I had cancer and was on one final pilgrimage of fornication.

'I must be three times your weight.'

'More, I hope.'

The mention of illness backfired, got her thinking about STDs, so in the end I went for honesty.

'I need to know what it feels like,' I said.

She wouldn't have sex, but was solicitous enough to roll about naked on top of me, my frail body barely able to support her.

I e-mailed Gillian the new chapters.

*

Editors are like headmasters, I discovered, in that they call you into their office a lot.

'Are you sure you're not having a breakdown? Change of career. Change of name.'

'I've just never liked David.'

'So we're to call you Will now?'

'Will Reed.'

'Have you looked in the mirror lately?'

'Is that a song lyric?'

'I'm sorry, David...'

'Will.'

'It's just not working out. You can see the week out in the newsroom – you can't interview people looking like that.'

This was fine. It took me ahead a few chapters – to where Will loses his job – before I'd had sex with a colleague, but I sought insight rather than replication. However, I was still eager to recreate Chapter Ten's strong dénouement. I walked to my desk, lifted the monitor up in order to throw it through the window. My mistake was obvious. In my description I had it detaching from the other hardware easily, before ending up in the car park two floors below. In reality the cables held it in place like guy ropes and so I placed it back down, Gillian's voice in my head waxing indignant about verisimilitude. I settled for shoving everything to the floor and made a mental note to revise the scene.

*

After being fired, Will descends into recreational drugs. He figures it's essential to embarking on a creative path. Literature, he decides, should be born of a reckless devotion to euphoria and its pursuit. Everything from rapture to depravity must be tasted and experienced in all its splendour and misery – a bank of sensations to withdraw from when needed.

He scores off a stranger in the pub – a nod, a wink and to the gent's for a furtive exchange – but after a fruitless night in the town's less salubrious establishments I knew this would also have to be rewritten. In the end a friend of a friend gave me her friend's number and told me to text for a rendezvous.

Will's language as he gets stoned came easily enough from personal experience, but my descriptions of his cocaine and heroin consumption were, shamefully, Googled for. (Chat rooms and blogs with exchanges of narcotic experiences are ubiquitous, with users comparing highs and comedowns; I'd simply amalgamated a few.)

The gram of coke in my inside pocket made me feel like a mischievous schoolboy all the way home in the taxi. I began with a few small lines over an hour or so, editing the relevant chapter as I observed myself. If anything I'd overstated the language, for there was no obvious intoxication, no clear transition from straight to high. I just felt a warmth, a sense of near bliss. As I wrote, everything was lucid and beyond the need for revision. I typed the keys like a concert pianist, yielding sublime, mesmeric prose. This wasn't work, it was my essence expressing itself. Will was almost certainly one of the great characters in literature. I snorted some more, stayed up working on the manuscript until dawn before sleeping lightly for a few hours. A profuse lethargy held me for most of the next day, but otherwise I felt fine.

I knew heroin was going to be different.

*

The shoplifting was easier than I thought, making me wonder why I had ever paid for anything. The trick appeared to be in your body language: maintaining a sanguine, guilt-free posture whilst smiling effusively at staff as you left the shop usually sufficed. Only once did I have to sprint away, pursued by a tenacious but fortunately rotund store detective.

Tattoos, though, hurt more than the hot scratch I'd described. The man inflicting the pain told me I'd chosen a particularly sensitive area for such a skinny person. I told him Will had chosen it to impress a woman, which left him looking unimpressed.

My dealer was unsurprised to see me back so soon, but thought my progression along the chemical spectrum a little alacritous.

'You go easy with this, my friend,' he said.

In my ignorance, I had assumed Will injected, and as I tied the tourniquet above my elbow and searched for a willing vein, I began to wish he'd smoked or snorted it. The sienna powder had been reluctant to dissolve, so I'd added a few drops of lemon juice, which renders it PH neutral, a trick Will didn't know about. After heating the underside of the spoon, I could draw the liquid into the syringe. I then flicked the barrel and expelled any air. I eased the needle's bevelled tip into a vein at forty-five degrees and pulled back the plunger a little, bringing up a small plume of puce into the brown. I removed the tourniquet with my teeth, pressed the plunger home and lay back.

The next day, when I'd finished being sick, I e-mailed Gillian the new version.

*

Spending a night in a cell didn't concern me unduly; what Will did to get there did. I had never hit anyone before, let alone been struck myself beyond scraps at school. I'd asked my estranged brother to punch me, but he'd just returned from a retreat and said it would unbalance his chi. Me hitting him was also out of the question.

Will argues with some men across a pool table before a fight starts – a lazy cliché now that I read it back. In the Mermaid I challenged the winner to a game and he obliged. As he cued I appraised his shot selection with derisive tuts, I took an age when it was my turn and then denied fouling a ball, but they seemed to allow men with pin heads for pupils and pin cushions for arms a certain dispensation. They even offered to buy me a drink and someone handed me a leaflet about rehab.

The Cow and Plough looked more promising. It had no pool table but several men were sat alone on stools with a do-not-disturb posture. The first was listing badly and barely registered my diatribe. Further along I found a more willing research assistant.

'You only hate them,' I said, 'because deep down you wonder what it's like to have a cock inside you.'

Despite inviting the punch, it still surprised me. There was none of the whip-crack you hear in films, no *kapow* or *phwack* from cartoon bubbles. Just a silent jolt, a sickening judder as my head swam about. I clamoured for adjectives, checked the sensations. And then I launched myself at him. No technique, no grace, just limbs whirling out of pure hatred. Few connected, and I took some more strikes, but the adrenaline flushing through me was rivalling the stuff I'd snorted and stuffed into my veins.

The next morning the duty solicitor came into my cell to advise me they were going to charge me with common assault.

'It needs to be ABH,' I rasped through a distended top lip.

*

The heroin was doing two things: assisting my weight loss further whilst ensuring no woman would look upon me as reasonable sexual material. The fight had also given my face several new shades and claimed three teeth. And anyway, conventional seduction was now beyond me.

My advert, although sounding extreme as I typed it, felt tepid once it was posted among the others on the website. I set a lower limit of twenty stones, alluded to what I'd be prepared to pay, logged off and gorged myself on Bach whilst shooting up.

As I slumped back on the sofa I could just make out the answer-phone kicking in and Gillian's voice: *Hi David. Love the new chapters. So visceral. So real. Call me. Ciao.*

*

There were no scales in the house but as I stood in front of the bedroom mirror I reckoned I'd lost half my body weight. Ribs protruded from my concave chest; I could almost push a finger in behind them. My legs were barely broader than the bone. Skin stretched across my sinews and joints, which looked like they might cut through it at any time. I was certainly smaller.

My height still troubled me, though, but there seemed little I could do about it. Amputation had an unrivalled permanence to it.

*

As I waited for her to arrive, I began to wonder what came next. There were no more instructions. No plot constructed beyond tonight's gore. The manuscript seemed to cover the floor of every room now and it took me ages to gather all the pages of Chapter Fourteen. I reminded myself of the detail before some last minute preparation.

*

I opened the door. She was enormous.

'Hi,' I said. 'I'm Will.'

'I'm…'

'Rapunzel,' I said. 'You're Rapunzel.'

Charlie's Afternoon

Ginny Baily

There was a step up to the path at number nine and Charlie didn't know how to manoeuvre the wheels of his new walker onto it`. It seemed too heavy to lift. He paused at the gate thinking someone might come out, examining the next door garden while he stood there, as if he'd only come out for a look at the flowers. It was a good garden, bursting with spring blooms. It put his own to shame. Not to mention number nine's dandelion crop. Charlie'd tended his garden for over sixty years, but he'd had to stop. He couldn't complain. He'd had sixty years.

It started to rain quite hard while Charlie stood at the gate of number nine and the cluster of scarlet tulips he'd been eyeing flapped as they were spattered with rain drops like agitated ladies who couldn't wait to be asked to dance. He'd forgotten his hat. He'd only thought to pop in and ask Terry if he could pick up the prescription from the chemist. He didn't need a hat for that. He held on to the gate with one hand and gave the frame of the walker a jerk with the other. The front wheel reared up but then came back to rest on the pavement. He saw he would need to push as well and the timing would need to be right. He ran through the sequence of movements in his head and then he tried again and the walker flipped up onto the path with Charlie in its wake. It was a good technique, but his wrist ached. He rang the doorbell.

They didn't have net curtains at number nine so Charlie could see into the living room and the empty armchair where Terry sat to watch the TV. Terry worked at home, so he was usually in. What exactly Terry did for a living was a mystery. Terry might have explained at some time what his profession was and why Charlie's garage was so crucial to its success, but Charlie might not have been listening or he might not have heard properly. That was more likely because the effectiveness of Charlie's ears was in inverse proportion to their size, or that's how it seemed. 'If they get any bigger,' he thought, 'I'll be stony deaf.'

Ivy said Terry was a good-for-nothing. She said he never drew his curtains so you could see him lolling in front of the television at all hours and his house smelt of cat's pee even though he didn't own a cat. But Charlie and Terry had a business arrangement. Man to man. Rain trickled down Charlie's nose, dripping onto his chin. A drop hung there. Terry was out.

Getting down the little step was no problem at all. Charlie paused by the gate and let the rain fall on his unprotected head while he chased an errant thought. Eventually, he caught it. He didn't need Terry. He could go himself, whatever the weather.

Should he go home and fetch his hat first, he wondered. It was only three doors back but it was the opposite direction, that was the thing. He was out now, he couldn't be going the wrong way. He could have sat by the gas fire in the front room to dry out a bit but he shook his head and turned stiffly away from home. He set off towards the main road in a street turned steamy grey. He went past the other houses, all quiet and locked up for the day, the occupants busy elsewhere, except for the cats sitting at windows. A tabby, perched on the sill below a 'Neighbourhood Watch' sticker, observed Charlie's slow progress with a fierce gleam. A ginger one's eyes were slit-shut but it twitched as he passed, as if Charlie were trespassing on its furry dreams.

Near the end of his street, a shape draped in red shot by shouting something at him as it swooped round the corner. It had vanished completely before he understood the words, 'Wet enough for you, Charlie?' It was the lady from number five. 'Too wet for me', he might have rejoined, but she'd gone. She was too fast on her bicycle in her red raincoat and he was too slow.

He turned the corner and looked up the hill. The rain made the hill look steeper than usual. 'Here we go,' he thought and put his head down to climb the slope. He was glad number five hadn't stopped or he might have been tempted to ask her to go to the chemist and that wasn't on because they didn't have a reciprocal business arrangement such as he had with Terry. He wasn't beholden. Ivy didn't know the half of it. It was mutually beneficial. Charlie handed over the garage key to Terry and in exchange Terry was available 'night or day, Charlie mate, night or day' to fetch a bit of shopping, run errands. And it wasn't as if he and Ivy were going to use the garage for anything else now.

'What's he keeping in there, dead animals?' Ivy had scoffed and she was right; it had reeked. You could smell it out in the back lane. But Charlie had had a word and Terry had sorted it out.

'Thanks for alerting me to that, Charlie mate,' he'd said, tapping his nose and raising a knowing eyebrow at Charlie as if they shared a secret. He never said what the smell was and Charlie hadn't asked.

Charlie wouldn't have rested until the top of the hill but there were people at the bus stop blocking the pavement and he couldn't see how to forge a passage so he waited with them, on the edge of their huddled umbrellas.

'Good morning Mr Hall,' a man said to him. He was better equipped for the rain than Charlie. Underneath his black umbrella he was wearing a smart bottle green mac that looked brand new. Charlie couldn't place him.

'How are you?' Charlie asked.

'Well!' said the man, as if Charlie had said something quite unexpected. He thought about the question a moment. Then he put his free hand on Charlie's arm and leaned toward him. 'Between you and me,' he whispered, 'Absolutely marvellous. Never been better.' The man squeezed Charlie's arm and turned away to fold up his umbrella because the bus had come.

Charlie took a moment to fish his hanky from his pocket and wipe his dripping nose and stretched his mind onto the walk ahead, pushing it round the corners and across the two main roads and all the way to the row of chairs in the chemist where you could sit while they got the prescription ready.

'Need a hand Gramps?' the bus driver called, but Charlie was thinking of the chairs in the chemist and of sherbet lemons. Ivy liked sherbet lemons.

*

Charlie had no idea how he'd got on the bus or where he was going. He smeared a space on the window to look out. The terraced houses set back from the road looked faintly familiar but wrong, like houses in a dream. They reminded him of the town he'd been stationed in at the end of the war. His hand on the wet glass was shaking and he put it on his knee next to the other one and held himself very still as the bus rumbled on through the unknown town. He stared down at his restless speckled old hands quivering like injured birds on his trouser legs. They provided no clues. When he dared to look out of the window again, he saw the cinema and that it was his own town where he had lived since he was quite a young man. His heart slowed down in his chest and he smiled at the Methodist chapel as they passed as at an old friend, although he hadn't been there for years. The bus would be at the city centre soon and he could go to the chemist in the High Street, he thought, remembering in a rush that he had been on his way to the chemist.

He noticed now that he was sitting in the seat reserved for the elderly and the disabled. He wondered at himself. He read the sign twice and shook his head in brisk little jerks so people would know he was not in the habit of usurping a seat kept for those less fortunate.

He watched the man with the green mac alight at the library. He looked very like Bernard who used to come round with the library van, but more colourful and younger.

The driver was humming an Irish tune that reminded him of the melody in the music box in his mother's front room. The parlour, she'd called it. You put a little key in the bottom of the box and wound it up. When you opened the lid the song flew wistfully out as if it longed to be allowed to float free and return home. 'Danny boy,' he said out loud and the driver half turned and flashed him a quick smile. She was just a slip of a girl. He tapped the beat of her tune on his good knee and realised it was nothing like Danny boy. It was probably a pop song. He looked again out of the window.

When the bus turned into the High Street, Charlie started to worry about how he was going to get off. The step was too high for him. And how would he walk even if he managed to alight? A blind panic invaded him and he stared straight ahead seeing not the road and the traffic but himself sprawled on the pavement, a tangle of powdery old bones. He pressed his lips together to keep from shouting. Then he gathered himself up, calling his strength and dignity into a solid ball of intent. He grasped the pole in front and heaved to his feet. He inched into the aisle. Other people started standing up too, crowding the aisle behind him but he couldn't be thinking about all of them. Nor of their need for him to shift before they could leave.

The bus stopped and the driver, still humming, whisked out of her seat, and pulled Charlie's Zimmer frame from the luggage rack where he now saw it had been all the time, nestling next to two folded pushchairs. He watched in wonder as she set it down on the pavement and flicked a pushchair erect on either side so the three wheeled contraptions stood in a line with the younger ones flanking his own like sentries. She hopped back onto the bus and gripped his upper arm firmly. He could feel the bruises forming and knew it would be purple by tea-time, but he didn't care. A moment later he was on the pavement, reunited with his walker. Along with the toddlers now strapped into their pushchairs and the toddlers' mothers, he was part of a sort of informal farewell committee. The driver waved at them all, her motley brood.

'Ta ta Gramps,' she shouted. 'Have fun!'

Then the bus had gone and Charlie was standing alone on the High Street in the heart of the city centre where he hadn't been for many months, not since before the operation. The rain had stopped and now the sun slid out from behind a cloud and sent its warmth down onto his head so he could feel his hair drying and his scalp warming. A heady surge of devil-may-care triumph swept through him and he hung on to the walker's frame, waiting for it to subside. He had the sensation of being a watery reed in the centre of a stream as people flowed past him on either side. He stood his ground. There never used to be so many people.

Eventually, the current tugged at him too and he shuffled along the sunny street with other people eddying around and past him but not bothering him in any way. He seemed to glide through the open door of the tobacconist shop where, because there was a queue, he took a seat at the little round table and breathed in the aromatic air, stretching his bad knee out to the side. His eye travelled over the comforting jars of tobacco on the shelf-lined walls and came to rest on the table top contents; an ashtray, a stack of pipe cleaners and several packets of matches with the name of the shop and a picture on the front. The picture showed this identical table. If Charlie had been there at the right time, he could have featured on the front of the matchbox. He would have needed his pipe to make the picture convincing. He patted his pipe pocket, but it was empty.

'Can I help you?' A thin young man stood before him, seeming almost to bow.

'I can't find my pipe,' said Charlie.

'Was it this week's special you wanted? The Widecombe mixture?'

Charlie, still patting his empty pocket as if he were calming his racing heart, gazed up at the young man.

'Or there's a deal on the Kentucky blend.'

'Kentucky?' said Charlie, shaking his head. He remembered the derby when he'd bet ten bob to win and lost the lot. Ivy had been mad at him. She'd never liked him smoking or gambling.

'Is there a betting shop near here?' asked Charlie but the shop assistant had disappeared. Charlie blinked at the place where he'd been.

An older man with a moustache and a tiny little beard came along. 'How are you sir? We haven't seen you for a long time.'

Although the doctor wouldn't have said such a thing because he saw Charlie quite regularly, the man sounded very like Dr Turner at the surgery. There was something both reassuring and commanding in his presence. Next thing the man would be asking him to pop up on to the table and slip his shirt off. Charlie nearly snickered but he saw the man's serious air, the way in which he humbly proffered something on his upturned palm. The phrase 'Hoskins, purveyors of the finest tobacco for three generations' played in his mind and he recalled a smoky event when the shop had re-opened after refurbishment. 'You look more like your father with that beard,' he said, pleased to repay Mr Hoskins' remembering with his own. Charlie glanced down at the offering, a familiar packet in red and gold. He gazed longingly and then reached out with the feeling that he was about to pluck forbidden fruit. 'That's my tobacco,' he said, his hand hovering between them.

'Yes sir.'

Charlie's other hand took tremulously to the air and grasped the first, tugging it down to his lap. He pursed his lips and looked down.

'Can I interest you in something else sir?' Mr Hoskins's voice was subdued.

Charlie was sorry to disappoint him but not as sorry as he was to disappoint himself. 'I don't smoke any more,' he whispered. 'It was me or the pipe.' He sighed deeply.

'You made the right choice,' said Mr Hoskins. 'Business is not what it used to be. We've had to diversify.' He flapped his hand vaguely in the direction of various exotic pipes and hubbly bubblies.

Charlie, all of a sudden acutely aware that he'd been availing himself of the comforts of the shop and offering no prospect of a sale in exchange, pulled his walker toward him.

'Are you in a hurry?' asked Mr Hoskins.

'I have to get to the chemist,' said Charlie, once again recalling the purpose of his outing, 'pick up my wife's prescription.'

'I just wondered if you would be willing to do me a favour,' said Mr Hoskins. 'It will only take two minutes.'

Charlie sat more upright and assumed an alert and curious air when Mr Hoskins returned with a small tray bearing jars with lids in different colours, pink and brown and pale orange. 'We are introducing our own blend,' he confided, 'feedback from a former smoker and connoisseur would be invaluable.'

Charlie solemnly lifted each lid in turn and sniffed at their enticing but indistinguishable contents. While he did so, Mr Hoskins expounded on the differing proportions of Burley, Virginia, Latakia and rarest Yenidje contained in each mixture.

'I like this one best,' Charlie said, pointing to the first jar he'd sampled. A comment bobbed up among the flotsam floating on the surface of his mind and he spoke it. 'Honey blonde,' he said, 'and spicy.'

Mr Hoskins beamed and inclined his head. 'You have a discerning nose.'

*

Charlie went smiling along the street and then the rain started splashing down on him again, although the sun was still shining. He sheltered under the awning of a department store and examined the window display. There was a sale on in the menswear department and he stepped inside, more to get out of the wet than anything else.

The lift was at the back of the store, a heavy old lift with fretworked doors. There used to be a person in this lift wearing a uniform and pressing the buttons importantly for the customers, but now they expected you to manage it all yourself. Charlie's finger was wavering in the vicinity of the controls when a red-faced woman with a small child on reins hurtled in. The child thrust himself in between Charlie and the controls, jabbing his podgy little fingers towards them, but unable to reach because his mother was holding him back, clutching at the reins as if she were hanging on to the horns of a rampaging bull and might at any moment be trampled.

'No,' she hissed at the child through clenched teeth. Charlie shook his head deferentially and indicated with a little nod that he was willing to forego his button pressing rights. The child bucked and snorted, flapping his arms in a frenzied attempt to reach.

'Let him press the button if he likes,' said Charlie, when the woman ignored his mute offer.

There was a pause in which Charlie held his gentlemanly stance, the woman stared stonily ahead, her face colouring darker and the child continued to thrash. Suddenly, in a deft movement, tugging the child towards her with her right hand while simultaneously reaching over his head and punching at the buttons with her left, the woman hit first the door-closing and then the second floor button in rapid succession. As the doors purred closed, the child set up a high pitched wail. Charlie hung his head, taking shallow breaths of the jagged noise-filled air. His knees were trembling. He kept his eyes averted as the woman exited, yanking the child along behind her. In his haste to ward off further intruders he pushed the wrong button and had a solitary detour to the top floor, in which the memory of his words to the tobacconist, 'honey blonde and spicy,' returned to him, lewdly.

There was quite a selection of the kind of caps he favoured in the sale. He tried on a checked tweed one. He was looking at the effect in the mirror when he realised someone was standing behind him and slightly to one side. He switched his focus to the other person and saw it was a woman with fuzzy brown hair who was regarding his reflection as intently as he had been a moment before. Her head leaned quizzically to one side and her hands were clasped in front. She did not meet his gaze in the mirror but ran her eye instead over his whole person. Charlie shivered at the familiarity with which she did this. Suddenly, she made a decision, stepped up behind him and plucked the cap from his head. Charlie kept very still. He watched her peer inside the cap as if he'd been hiding something in there and he wanted to protest. She looked at him in the mirror then and she tutted and frowned as if someone ought to have known better. She disappeared taking Charlie's new cap with her and he went on standing in front of his own reflection, looking at the inverse world behind. After a while the woman returned and replaced the hat on his head.

'Got the right size this time,' she said. 'I think that really suits you.' She adjusted the cap as if he were a schoolboy and she his mother. She set it at a jaunty angle like a French onion seller's beret. 'Oh, you'll turn a few heads wearing that,' she said and snorted with laughter. She clamped her hand over her mouth to hold her merriment in, inviting Charlie with little nods and eyebrow twitches to join in.

'Do you have any cloth caps?' he asked coldly. 'The weather's too warm for tweed.'

'It'd do for winter too,' she said defensively, but he raised an eyebrow, implying that neither of them could possibly know whether one as ancient as he would be around to sport such headgear come the winter. Chastened, the woman bowed her fuzzy head in acknowledgement and fetched him a navy blue cloth cap. She apologised that it was the only one left. There'd been such a rush on them because they were half price. She pointed out that it had waterproof coating and little air vents so his scalp wouldn't overheat. She placed it in his hand so he could don it himself and offered him a further discount because of an invisible fault in the stitching.

'I'll take it,' said Charlie. 'It matches my Zimmer frame.' He flashed his dentures at her to show it was a joke and she again pressed her hand to her mouth to dampen the mirth that warbled out between her fingers. He didn't need a bag. He wore his new cap straightaway.

*

Not long afterwards he was surprised to hear someone calling his name and Charlie, looking around, saw he was at the end of the High Street, almost at the roundabout. Terry from number nine was shouting from his car, offering Charlie a lift.

It was double yellow lines so Terry put his hazard warning lights on. 'You're a long way from home Charlie,' he said, taking Charlie's walker from him and helping Charlie position himself for entry into the passenger seat.

'What am I doing here?' he asked but Terry didn't hear. He was trying to squeeze Charlie's walker into the box-filled boot. Just as well because Charlie remembered at that moment about the chemist. He must have walked straight past. He explained to Terry that he should have gone to the chemist, but Terry was distracted by the traffic building up behind them. He wanted Terry to say, like he sometimes did, 'I wouldn't worry Charlie mate, we all forget things sometimes. I'd forget my own head if it wasn't screwed on.' He told Terry that it was just Ivy's usual high blood pressure pills, nothing to worry about or anything, but she needed them today because she'd nearly run out.

There was a lorry unloading on the other side of the road and no one could get past while Charlie tried to manoeuvre himself into the car. He lowered himself bottom first onto the passenger seat. Then he had to swing his legs in but his right knee didn't easily bend beyond a certain angle these days. The driver of the car behind beeped his horn.

'No hurry Charlie, you take your time,' Terry said. 'Don't worry about these half-wits.' Other drivers joined in the cacophony. Terry went to the back of the car and shouted at them. 'Fucking chill out,' he shouted. 'Can't you see he's a disabled geriatric?'

Charlie forced his knee to fold like one of those collapsing pushchairs and fumbled to strap himself in before the burning sensation paralysed him in its grip. His knee joint was a dark and dusty cavern where a bonfire blazed.

'Some people!' said Terry, when they finally got going. 'No respect.'

Knee-tortured, Charlie was speechless.

'No fucking karma, that's their problem. Excuse my French,' said Terry, glancing across at Charlie who managed a grunt. It was enough and Terry looked back at the road, concentrating on the traffic and explaining his karmic transference theory. Charlie subsided into sleep. In his dream he was trying to climb a steep slope but something was holding him back. He was tethered. He awoke as the car pulled up outside the local chemist, the one two streets away from home. He had slumped down as if some bones had been removed while he dozed so that only the seat belt was preventing him from slithering to the car floor.

Terry had stopped on double yellow lines again. He left the engine running. 'You sit there Charlie mate while I nip in. Sweet talk the traffic warden for me.'

Charlie levered himself up to a proper sitting position. He admired his new cap in the mirror. 'Discerning nose,' he thought and smiled. He'd tell Ivy. 'Oh, sherbet lemons,' he remembered, guiltily. Terry swung back in.

'Five to ten minute wait,' he said, darting into a recently-freed parking space. The woman who'd been patiently waiting to occupy it shouted soundlessly from her car. 'Good for her karma,' said Terry and shot off again before Charlie could mention the sweets.

The car clock said four. Charlie might be back in time for Ivy waking up from her nap. He could do with a nap himself. He didn't know when he'd been so tired. He leaned back against the head-rest and closed his eyes. She was partial to a sherbet lemon after a cup of tea. Charlie's eyes popped open and he swallowed nervously, overwhelmed by a sense of his own impending audacity. He looked at the newsagents across the road and he made his decision.

He opened the door and put his left leg, his good leg, out. Gently he lifted the right one with both hands, swivelled it in its locked position out the door and slowly stretched it. The knee bonfire blazed again and he waited for it to die down. Then he gripped the handle above the door with one hand and the top of the door itself with the other and pulled himself upright, switching his left hand to the car roof as he rose. As soon as his legs seemed ready to take more weight, he gripped the rim of the roof with both hands and crept sideways so he could push the door closed. When he let go, he swayed.

Taking tiny paces and leading always with his good leg, Charlie advanced on the zebra crossing. He seemed to gather momentum as he progressed so that he had to grasp the belisha beacon at the kerbside to prevent himself from tipping into the road before he was ready. The cars stopped but still he took another moment to get his breath and steady himself. And then he was off again, shuffling across like a tightrope walker, his arms fluttering low next to his sides for balance, his head ringing with giddiness, lightly touching the post on the other side as if he were clocking in but not stopping, now he'd found a rhythm, sweeping on relentlessly along the far pavement and through the door of the newsagent, which emitted an electronic beep as he entered, a tuneless fanfare to his achievement, and arriving at the counter, which he grasped. He held on, his heart a tremble.

The girl behind the counter was talking to someone on a mobile phone. Charlie waited for her to notice him. She was wearing tight jeans and a short t-shirt which left her flat brown tummy bare. Just as well Ivy wasn't with him or she'd have something to say about young women being slaves to fashion and the risk of catching a chill on their unprotected kidneys. Charlie admired the girl's long shiny black hair and the soft curve of her bare shoulders. 'Shazia!' a voice rang out and Charlie almost jumped. He hadn't realised anyone else was there. A solid older woman in a green and gold sari was sitting on a stool further along the counter. She'd been busy sorting magazines into piles but now was frowning at Charlie. He saw the magazines had photographs of large-breasted women on the covers and quickly looked away.

'A quarter of sherbet lemons please,' he said.

'Yeah, yeah. Too right,' the girl said as she reached up to the shelf behind and lifted down the jar. The mobile phone clenched between her hunched shoulder and her ear, she kept up her assenting mutter as she shook the sweets into the scales. A jewel in the side of her nose glinted. 'Hundred grams, was it?' she mumbled. Charlie thought she was talking to the other person and didn't answer. 'Hundred grams, was it?' she repeated in a firm, loud voice.

Charlie tried to remember what that meant. 'Better make it two hundred,' he said, 'to be on the safe side.'

Clutching the rather large bag of sherbet lemons, Charlie made his way back to the car, stopping to rest only once. Terry hadn't yet returned. Once he had inserted himself into the passenger seat and strapped himself in, he opened the white paper bag and looked with satisfaction at the mound of sweets glistening there, acid yellow and almost luminous. There were plenty. He popped one into his mouth and closed his eyes. His tongue probed a crack in the hard sugary surface and the crack became a fissure. The sherbet centre burst onto his tongue with a fizz of sweetness and a memory assailed him as if it had been hidden inside. He recalled himself as a young man, on his way to pick Ivy up from her house to take her to the pictures. She lived at the bottom of a long hill and he was worried about being late so he started to run. He ran with big bounding strides like a giant down the Halliwell Road, the bag of sherbet lemons that was to be the first present he ever gave her tucked into his breast pocket, one stolen sweet bulging in his cheek. The air rushed past as he sped onwards and ever downward, his knees chopping the air, his feet pounding the pavement. He could have run forever.

*

'Where've you been?' Ivy said when he arrived home. 'What's that contraption on your head?' She'd expected him half an hour before and the tea had stewed. 'Been rollicking about with that ne'er-do-well have you?' she said.

Charlie settled down on the sofa while she made a fresh pot. He smiled to himself, fingering the sherbet lemons in his pocket.

My Giant Tongue

Luke Kennard

My large white coffee was served in a cup so wide the liquid had immediately fallen to room temperature and slapped annoyingly over the sides whenever I picked it up or my knee nudged the nearest leg of the wobbly aluminium table.

I was staring at a girl on the other side of the room, sitting below a tapestry depicting the transformation scene from *A Midsummer Night's Dream*. She was knitting or crocheting or something, drawing from a bright red ball of wool under her chair. The girl could have fitted into a small suitcase. She had the pale, waxy face of a china doll, a horse's tail of long black hair, a little red mouth and bright blue eyes. A large, painful-looking spot on her cheek was the only human feature, although it just made her look like a china doll with a disfiguring spot carefully sculpted on its cheek. She looked up from her knitting and noticed me. I jerked away, spilling more coffee from my big shallow cup, as if her look had stung me.

In the absence of a book or a newspaper I pretended to study the menu's florid descriptions of sandwich fillings, but I could tell she was still watching. I put down the menu.

'What's that you're making?' I said.

She looked me in the eye.

'Your tongue,' she said harshly and went back to knitting it.

I stood up, dashing the last of the coffee from its cup. I went to her table and tried to make myself look tall.

'What's your name?' I said,

'Gloria Victoria,' she said, without looking up. She said it in a horrible singsong voice which suggested Gloria Victoria was not really her name at all.

The scarf she was knitting was long with a groove running down the centre.

'My tongue, eh?' I said. 'Fancy that.'

Gloria Victoria continued to knit furiously, her needles clicking like an insect. She was only a little girl, really – and I started to feel bad for standing over her like that. I paid for my breakfast, added a pound tip for the waiter and left the café.

*

I kicked through the pigeons to the taxi rank, stopping at my usual stall to pick up a copy of *The Times*.

'I think I leave soon,' said Mikhailos, giving me my change. '*Rain* for *two weeks*.'

I tried to say 'Thank you,' to Mikhailos, but my tongue felt too fat for my mouth and it came out as one long lisp. I had to repeat my place of work three times to the cab driver. As I clambered into the back seat, I laughed and apologised. I would have explained about the girl in the café and how it was probably psychological, but the thought of trying to say "probably psychological" with my swollen tongue made me wince.

*

By the time I reached the office my mouth was full of my tongue and I could barely make a sound. This troubled me as I was supposed to be giving a press conference today. 'Uh pweth gontherenth,' I said out loud. I took a card from the receptionist's desk and wrote:

My tongue has swollen up. Do you have anything which might be good for that, e.g. paracetamol or ibuprofen?

I sat at my desk and checked my e-mails. Catherine brought me a glass of water and two red capsules.

'Thah hoo,' I said.

With some prising and gurning I managed to get the pills down. Fifteen minutes later my tongue was bigger still. I e-mailed Daniels.

You may need to give the press conference in my place, Daniels, I wrote. *My tongue has swollen to an enormous size and I can't speak. I think I may have to go home.*

A couple of minutes later Daniels appeared at my desk.

'Alright, Steve?' he said.

I shrugged.

'You can't say a word?'

I opened my mouth to say, 'No,' but instead my tongue popped out, rolled up like a liquorice ribbon or a tape measure and proceeded to spool down my chest and onto the computer keyboard. Throughout this I was making a 'Gurrrrurrrrurrrrr,' sound. My tongue, now around three feet long, lay twitching in a heap on my computer keyboard.

Daniels just stood there looking appalled.

'Catherine?' he called, backing away from my desk.

'Yeah?' said Catherine, approaching. 'You're lucky I'm here to solve all your – Oh my God, your *tongue*, Stephen!'

I nodded.

The tongue started dancing around on the keyboard. It was still my tongue, all the way down my throat, but it was moving of its own accord. I stared at it, wide-eyed.

'*Mate!*' said Daniels, beaming. He took out his mobile phone.

'He's trying to type something,' said Catherine.

I shook my head.

'Open Word!' said Catherine.

Daniels opened Word.

...Freeman and slave, patrician and plebeian, lord and serf, guild-master and journeyman, in a word oppressor and oppressed, stood in constant opposition to one another...

the tongue was typing. I grabbed it and pulled it from the keyboard. The tongue lashed about in my hands for a moment before settling around my neck like a scarf. Then it started to constrict. I rolled off my chair and onto the floor, clutching at my throat. Daniels yelped. Catherine tried to grab me by the shoulders.

'Loosen his shirt!' she shouted.

'What good's that going to do?' said Daniels.

Catherine tried to prize my tongue away from my neck, but it was wrapped twice and getting tighter. I thrashed out for the keyboard and managed to bring it to the floor. The tongue immediately relaxed, slithered around my throat twice, deleted the letters and numbers I'd hit while reaching for the keyboard and continued:

...carried on an uninterrupted, now hidden, now open fight, a fight that each time ended, either in a revolutionary reconstitution of society at large, or in the common ruin of the contending classes...

I gasped for breath as my tongue leaped from key to key.

'This calls into question every conclusion I've drawn from life so far,' said Daniels, gravely.

'What do we do?' said Catherine. 'Call an ambulance?'

The clock struck 10.

Immediately my tongue snapped straight and rolled back into my mouth, as if on a spring. I swallowed once and found that my tongue had returned to normal size.

'Ha!' I said, clearly. 'That's better.'

'Thank God,' said Catherine. 'Your poor tongue.'

'Hey,' said Daniels, 'I just Googled that passage: it's from a book called *The Communist Manifesto* by Karl Marx and,' Daniels wandered back to his computer, 'Friedrich Engels,' he called from the other side of the room.

'I know what it's from,' I said, crossly. 'What I want to know is: why was my tongue typing it.'

*

The café was empty, a different waiter manning the till. Had he seen a tiny knitting girl? He hadn't.

'Hey,' said Catherine, 'over here.'

A single strand of red wool was tied to the leg of the aluminium chair where Gloria Victoria had been sitting. The wool led out of the café and up the road.

'Quickly,' I said.

Catherine and I followed the red thread over the road, past the cinema and around a bus-stop. Daniels had stayed in the office to explain to the newspapers the dismantling of the free school bus service. What was extraordinary, Daniels would be saying, was that we had ever managed to offer a free school bus service at all, what with the impending recession.

The red thread came to an end outside an abandoned department store. The windows were plastered with day-glo posters for something called *THE 8TH DAY HOLY FREE CHURCH OF THE IMMACULATE TONGUE OF FIRE.*

Meeting daily this week for EMERGENCY PRAYER *SERVICES. Morning, noon and night. Open to members and inquisitives. Come on in!*

'Tongue!' I said. 'It's a clue!'

'I suppose so,' said Catherine. 'It doesn't look like anyone's here.'

I pushed the dirty glass door and it opened without effort. Inside the department store was dusty and silent, littered with crumbs of broken glass. Day-glo signs had been taped to the walls with big arrows pointing further into the building and up a broken-down escalator. There was a surprising distance between each step. We could hear music coming from behind a double door at the top.

*

The darkened hall was full to capacity with a seated audience. A brass band squawked atonally and seemed to be improvising. We occupied two seats in the front row. I sat next to a woman with enormous frizzy hair, staring placidly ahead. After a drum roll, a fat man in evening dress appeared on stage and began to stride up and down singing along to the band. I don't remember the verses, but the chorus was just:

Will ya miss me? Will ya miss me when I die?

over and over again. When he stopped there was a burst of recorded applause and cheering. The two hundred or so members of the congregation remained silent.

'Well,' said the fat man. 'for those of you new to this church, I'm Ranger Martin Julius.'

'Ranger?' Catherine whispered.

'And I'm here to welcome you today,' said Ranger Julius, 'whether you're joining us here at the Holy Free Church of the Immaculate Tongue of Fire for the first time, or whether this is your second or even third visit. Maybe you don't know *why* you came here today. Perhaps something just compelled you to enter the building and you've found yourself in the hall. Welcome. Maybe,' and here Ranger Julius looked directly at me, 'there's a very specific reason why you've come here. Maybe you'd like to come up and share with us.'

Catherine shoved my shoulder. I frowned at her, but saw that she had tears in her eyes.

'Go,' she said.

I put up my hand like a schoolboy as I stood and made my way to the stage, Ranger Julius grinning at me in encouragement. I felt dizzy as I climbed the stairs.

'What's your name, son?' he said.

'Stephen.' My voice was inexplicably high-pitched.

'And what are you, Stephen?'

'I…' I said. 'I'm a minor government clerk with the local council.'

'And what have you come to tell us?' asked Ranger Julius, projecting his question over the whole theatre.

I couldn't speak.

'Speak through him, Lord,' cried Ranger Julius. 'Oh, Lord, speak through your servant, Stephen.' He slammed me on the back.

I opened my mouth and my tongue fell out – longer than before, as long as a hose pipe. Then longer.

'Take up the tongue!' said Ranger Julius. 'Take it up and pass it around.'

I made hand gestures as if to say 'No! Don't!' but they were ignored. I stood mute as the tip of my tongue was picked up by a smartly dressed young man and passed through the first row, everyone singing, '*We will glorify this precious tongue.*'

My tongue was threaded through the whole auditorium until everybody had a hand on it. The taste of two hundred hands was extraordinary. When my tongue reached the end of the back row, Ranger Julius put his hand on my shoulder.

'Children,' said Ranger Julius. 'Is it not as I have promised you?'

My tongue went rigid and shot outwards, then constricted, sharply.

The congregation began to scream as my tongue hauled them towards me. I tried to apologise with my eyes – which were now sitting atop my cavernous maw and probably not even visible to the mob my tongue was reeling in. I spotted Catherine trying to wriggle free of the sinuous ribbons. I had a headache and closed my eyes. Every surface seemed suddenly to be very grimy, smeared with a dark paste which came to resemble the night sky. Amid the noise I could hear Ranger Julius half singing, half shouting, 'Just as I promised!' It was as if a bucket of stars had been knocked over, then everything became very clean, each colour impossibly uniform, eventually monochrome. I swallowed, once. The hall was empty.

'Hello?' I said.

*

Back at the office I checked my emails. No new messages.

'There you are,' said Daniels. 'How's it going?'

'Not so good, Daniels,' I said. 'I'm afraid I've eaten Catherine and a minor Pentecostal sect.'

'Minor to you, perhaps,' said Daniels, petulantly. 'I expect they saw themselves as the one true church.'

'That's hardly the point,' I snapped. Daniels had recently been sent on a religious sensitivity programme and had been a bit of a pill ever since.

'What will that tongue of yours do next?' Daniels wondered. 'It's attacked the state, the church... What do you think it's trying to tell us?'

The phone rang. Daniels answered.

'Yeah, he's here,' he said. 'It's for you.'

*

Cllr Archer McEwitt was a notorious malcontent. He was prone to organising emergency caucuses over trifling matters and I had grown accustomed to dozing through his interminable tirades. But this time Archer McEwitt had had enough.

'The only thing for it is to fire everyone and start from scratch. Dismantle them all. The universities, the banks, the farms. Everything. Including ourselves.'

This, I felt, revealed Archer McEwitt as the crazy extremist he was. I was horrified, then, to see my fellow councillors nodding in approval.

'Stephen here is different, though,' said Archer. 'Stephen and his tongue.'

I was seized with fear.

'I don't want it!' I said. 'I don't want your disapprobation *or* your approval! I don't want to care what you think about me!'

'The only worthy leader is one who refuses the honour,' said Archer.

Then Archer McEwitt painted a picture of a world in which there was only one substance: my tongue. Buses made of my tongue, tower blocks, the roads paved with tongue. The whole world reduced to a single, manageable muscle. 'And the tongue starts here,' said Archer. 'From this office.'

The entire room stared at me.

'Come on then,' said Archer, prodding me in the stomach. 'Out with it.'

Nothing happened.

'I don't know what he's talking about,' I said.

A discontented murmur.

'Oh come now,' said Archer. 'Don't try to deny it. We've got all the footage on camera.'

My tongue burst from my mouth and slithered around the room, surrounding my fellow councillors. In one fluid motion it gathered them into my mouth where I swallowed them all. I began to wonder if Archer McEwitt was right.

*

Outside it was still raining. I didn't know where I was going until I noticed Gloria Victoria on the other side of the road. She was even smaller than I remembered. About the size of a cat. I ran through the traffic and picked her up.

'What have you done?' I screamed over the traffic noise.

Gloria Victoria said 'Ma-ma!' in a mechanical voice. A doll.

I ate it.

I looked at the dual-carriageway, thick with vehicles, each with their drivers, with all their souvenirs and opinions. It gave me an idea.

*

'Harlech, Sunday Times,' said a young man with neat black hair. 'What was your reaction when you realised you could eat anything with the help of your enormous tongue?'

'A mixture of fear and incomprehension,' I said. 'Next.'

'Channel 4 news,' said a woman with *pince-nez* and a bob. 'What are you planning to eat next?'

'The M5,' I said. 'Then all other motorways, before moving onto A and then B roads.'

'Henderson, BBC. Why roads?'

'Because I think people should just stay where they are,' I said. 'Wasn't it Pascal who said …'

Before I could quote Pascal, my tongue rolled out of my mouth like a red carpet. It knocked everyone in the press conference off their feet and proceeded to juggle everything into the air, the cameras and the boom operators and the journalists. This time my tongue didn't stop growing. It breached the door and spread across the street. From the window I could see it wrapping all the way around a lamppost – like a fleshy ribbon around a maypole. Within seconds the lamppost was completely bound in my tongue. I lay on the stage like a fishing reel.

A few hours later Daniels brought me a laptop so I could communicate with the rest of mankind.

THANKS DANIELS, I typed. The caps lock was on, but that seemed like a relatively minor issue. HOW FAR'S IT GONE NOW?

'It's south of the river,' said Daniels. 'It's mummifying everything in its path. The police want to know what your terms are.' Daniels looked sheepish and scratched the back of his neck. 'They've tried to chop off your tongue...'

OH NO! I typed.

'But it just strangled them.'

YAY!

'So you're taking the tongue's side now?' Daniels wanted to know.

I DON'T SEE THAT I REALLY HAVE A CHOICE.

Writers

Ginny Baily is political editor of the Africa Research Bulletin and co-editor of Riptide short story journal. Her stories and poetry have appeared in a range of journals and anthologies such as 'Momaya', 'Wasafiri', the 'Warwick Review', 'Succour' and the forthcoming 'Tell Tales iv'. She is writing a novel set in West Africa and Devon.

Wendy Brandmark is a fiction writer, reviewer and lecturer. Her novel 'The Angry Gods,' was published in the UK and the US, and her short stories have appeared widely in anthologies and journals, including 'Critical Quarterly,' 'The Jewish Quarterly' and forthcoming issues of 'Short Fiction' and the 'Massachusetts Review'. She recently completed a collection of short stories with the support of an Arts Council writer's grant, and is currently working on a new novel.

Paul Brownsey was once a newspaper reporter and is now a philosophy lecturer at Glasgow University. His stories have been published in many journals in Britain, Ireland and North America. He has recent or forthcoming work in 'Staple' (England), 'Chiron Review' (U.S.A.), 'Wascana Review' (Canada) and 'Dalhousie Review' (Canada). He was runner-up in the 2007 Fish Publishing prize (Ireland).

John Burnside is a writer of poetry, short stories and novels who has received numerous awards. He teaches at the University of St Andrews. His most recent publications are 'The Devil's Footprints' (2007) and 'Glister' (2008). In 2008 he has also published a collection of lyric poetry, 'Goose Music',

Riptide Vol. 3

co-written with **Andy Brown**, Director of the Centre for Creative Writing and Arts at the University of Exeter.

Gordon Collins (www.zipple.co.uk) has been a market risk analyst, mathematician, computer graphics researcher, English teacher and inventor. He now lives in Norwich where he is finishing his first novel, 'Extremely Normal' and starting his second, 'Japanity.'

Kate Dunton is an Art Historian by training, but has recently reorganised her career in order to spend more time on her fiction writing. She has read at 'Tales of the Decongested' and has just started an MA in Novel Writing at City University. She lives in North West London.

Jane Feaver was born in Durham and now lives in North Devon. Her first novel, 'According to Ruth' was published by Harvill Secker in 2007. A collection of stories, 'Love Me Tender', will be published in 2009.

Penny Feeny is an award-winning short fiction writer, based in Liverpool, whose work has appeared internationally in print, on radio and online. Publication credits include 'Aesthetica', 'Atlantic Unbound', 'Crannog', 'Literary Mama', 'Mslexia', 'The Reader', 'Staple', and 'Tears in the Fence', as well as anthologies from 'Tindal Street', 'Route', 'Comma', and 'Accent Press'.

Sally Flint is a published writer of poetry and prose and is co-editor of Riptide. She is also a facilitator for 'Stories Connect' which helps ex-offenders and substance mis-users change their lives through literature. Her doctoral research involves examining contemporary ekphrastic practice in poetry. She was a runner up in the 2008 Bridport prize for poetry.

Liz Gifford has written for the 'Times' and 'Independent' newspapers, and has had poetry accepted by 'Cinnamon Press' and the 'Oxford Magazine'. She has been commissioned to write a book about China. She has completed a creative writing diploma at Oxford and is working on a novel, 'The Selkie', for the MA at Royal Holloway.

Luke Kennard is a poet and dramatist whose second collection of verse, 'The Harbour Beyond the Movie' (Salt Publishing) was shortlisted for the Forward Prize for Best Collection 2007. He lectures in creative writing at the University of Birmingham and is working on his first novel.

Tom J Vowler lives in Plymouth. His short stories have appeared in several publications including 'Brand', 'Cadenza' and 'Ink', as well as winning first prize in the 2008 HappenStance international story competition. On completion of an MA in creative writing Tom wrote a collection of short stories and has just started his second novel. More at www.tomvowler.co.uk